MURDER AT CORGI COUNTRY CLUB

A WAGGING TAIL COZY MYSTERY

CINDY BELL

CONTENTS

ISBN: 9781086882605

CHAPTER 1

Sparks of color scattered across the morning sky as Nikki Green parked in front of the animal shelter. Two other cars took up spaces in the large parking lot. The morning shift consisted of Petra, the manager of the shelter, and Grant, one of the employees. Nikki preferred to volunteer in the morning, as that seemed to be when the shelter needed the most help. As Nikki stepped out of her car, sharp barks rang through the air. Many people in the town of Dahlia were still sound asleep in their beds, but the animals inside the shelter were eager to start their day.

Nikki turned the key, that Petra had given her for her early morning visits, in the lock on the front door. The barking increased in reaction to the subtle clink of the door handle.

"Morning friends." Nikki smiled as she stepped into the lobby of the animal shelter. She turned the lock on the door behind her, then scrunched up her nose. A mixture of animal scents, as well as cleaner fumes combined to create a smell that only the animal shelter had. It wasn't exactly bad, but it wasn't exactly good either. Nikki adjusted to it as she headed down the hall to the kennels.

Although Nikki helped wherever help was needed, her heart did belong to the cats and dogs of the shelter. She would visit the cats and often she took the dogs for walks, or just out to play to give them a little exercise. Lately, her dog-walking business had picked up, and she hadn't been to visit as much. She vowed to correct that, as the shelter dogs and cats were just as important to her as the dogs she walked each day.

"Nikki, is that you?" A voice called out from the end of the long corridor that ran the length of the kennels. Although Nikki couldn't see the source of the voice, she recognized its sweet but frazzled tone.

"Yes, it's me, Petra. Good morning."

"Good morning. I'm so glad you're here. Can

you start on the food on that end? I'll meet you in the middle."

"Sure." Nikki's response was drowned out by the sound of a hose being turned on. Petra was a bit obsessive when it came to keeping the runs clean for the dogs. Nikki loved that about her. She made sure every animal in her care was not only safe and well cared for, but also loved.

"Hey there, Spots." Nikki crouched down in front of the first kennel and smiled at the Dalmatian. When he came in as a stray, one of the workers had begun calling him Spots, and the name stuck. "Nobody came to get you yet, huh?" She frowned as she reached through the bars to stroke his ears. "Don't worry, pal, someone is going to be so lucky to have you."

Nikki hoped that would be the case. Sometimes it was hard for her to see the animals at the shelter, and then go to the homes of animals that were very loved by their families. It didn't seem fair that some dogs had a safe and warm home to curl up each night, while others still waited to be welcomed into a family. At least she knew they were well cared for at the shelter.

As Nikki began to dish out food to each of the kennels, the dogs became even more excited. She laughed at their exuberance. When the cup she used to portion the food scraped the bottom of the large bag, she frowned.

"Hey Petra, you're getting pretty low on dog food." Nikki tossed a cupful of kibble into the bowl of a mixed Pointer, then looked up at her friend as she reached the next kennel.

"I know." Petra frowned as she looked down at the clipboard in her hand. Her fingers tightened along the edge of it. "I'm going to try to get some tomorrow."

"Try to?" Nikki met her eyes. "Do you need me to run to the store for you? I can pick it up later this afternoon."

"It's not that." Petra took a deep breath, her eyebrows furrowed as she looked back at Nikki. "Things are pretty tight right now. Of course, first priorities will be taken care of, such as food and other immediate needs. But honestly, I'm not sure the shelter will remain open after the end of the month. So many of our resources have run dry. Even the vet that allows us to make deferred payments, we're so far behind now that he can't continue to offer services." The breath she drew trembled a little, before she exhaled. "It's a tough time right now. If it weren't for volunteers like you, we wouldn't even still be running."

"Petra, I had no idea things had gotten so bad." Nikki frowned as she searched Petra's eyes. "Why didn't you tell me?"

"I thought I had a few more resources I could rely on, and when they fell through, I realized just how desperate we were." Petra wiped the back of her hand along her forehead and settled her tired gaze on Nikki. "I'll figure out something, I'm sure. I always do. It's just a little more dire than usual."

"If there's anything I can do to help, just let me know." Nikki frowned. She wished she could offer a generous cash donation, but there wasn't a lot of money in dog walking and pet sitting. It paid for her small apartment, and other needs, but it didn't leave her a lot to hand out. She had been saving to purchase a piece of land where she hoped to build a house and animal retreat. She hoped the retreat would include dog and cat boarding facilities, a rescue shelter and a small training facility. She could donate some of that money to help out. She just needed to work out how much.

"Nikki, you already do so much." Petra smiled and shook her head. "Don't you worry about this.

Thank you for letting me vent. Now, I know that Bassie needs a run. She's been whining all morning."

"I'll take her right out." Nikki stared at her a moment longer, as she searched her mind for a solution. A soft whine from Bassie's kennel drew Nikki farther down the corridor. The Corgi had been turned into the shelter as a senior dog, but she didn't act like one. She loved to run and play just like the puppies. As Nikki opened the kennel and crouched down to greet her, a rush of determination flooded through her. She would find a way to help Petra and the shelter, no matter what it took.

After exercising a few of the dogs and helping with some cleaning, Nikki dropped her car off at her apartment, then began to gather her dogs for their morning walk. Coco, a German Shepherd, greeted her at the door of his house with a drippy smile.

"Oh, I see you've already been in your water bowl." Nikki grinned as she crouched down to greet him. Although Coco's large size and strong frame intimidated some, Nikki knew he was a sweetheart that loved a hug. She put her arms around his shoulders and gave him a gentle squeeze, then clipped his leash on.

As Nikki worked her way through her collection of dogs, she used the time to consider options for the shelter. She could ask her clients for donations, but that wouldn't likely add up to much. The shelter needed a large infusion of cash, and fast.

Once Nikki had returned all of the dogs to their homes, she continued on her journey to her friend Sonia Whitter's house. Calling it a house was an understatement, it was a mansion, an estate, with one of the oldest and most valuable homes in Dahlia centered on several acres of property.

Nikki walked Sonia's Chihuahua, Princess at least once a day. She usually walked her with some of her other dogs, but a few times a week she walked her separately, and Sonia had started joining them. Though she was about fifty years older than Nikki, Sonia had become one of her closest friends, and they both enjoyed sharing the time together. However, that morning as she led Princess along the sidewalk, Nikki was distracted and couldn't bring herself to gossip about the latest controversy to hit the country club.

Nikki listened to the sound of her own footsteps, as well as Princess' tiny paws skittering across the pavement. The Chihuahua had more energy than most dogs she walked, and though her legs were tiny she could move very fast.

"Nikki, what's wrong?" Sonia glanced over at her as she stared down at the sidewalk.

"Huh?" Nikki looked over at Sonia and smiled as she shook her head. "I'm sorry, my mind is somewhere else. How have you been doing?"

"I asked you first." Sonia raised an eyebrow as she continued to study Nikki. "I know when something is up. You're never this quiet."

"You're right." Nikki sighed. "I'm not very good company today. I spent a few hours this morning at the animal shelter, and things are so stressful there right now. I just can't get it off my mind."

"Stressful? What do you mean?" Sonia snapped her fingers at Princess as the dog sniffed at the edge of a flower garden. "Not in Mr. Palo's flowers, Princess. No, no! I'll never hear the end of it." Sonia huffed and rolled her eyes.

"Over here, Princess." Nikki gently guided her to a patch of grass along the sidewalk. "Unfortunately, they haven't been able to keep up steady enough donations. It's possible the shelter might have to close by the end of the month. I just wish there was something more that I could do to help."

"Not enough donations?" Sonia waved her hand and laughed. "Oh, that's no trouble at all."

"What?" Nikki turned to face her. "What do you mean? Without donations they can't buy supplies, or continue to pay the vet that treats the animals."

"What I mean is, that's a problem we can fix." Sonia fished her phone out of her purse. "I'll just make a few phone calls and we'll have a fundraiser set up in no time."

"A fundraiser?" Nikki's eyes widened. "I don't know why I didn't think of that."

"Maybe because you don't have years of experience running them." Sonia put her phone to her ear. "Don't worry, I have every contact I need to get everything going. I also have some things I am happy to donate. We can have it at the country club, they love anything that gets their name in the paper." She held up her finger and turned her attention to her phone. "Gloria? Oh wonderful, yes. Listen, I'd like to throw a party, are you up for it?" She laughed at the response. "I thought you would be. It's for the local animal shelter. Yes, and it needs to be put together as quickly as possible. Say, this Sunday?" She paused, glanced at Nikki, then smiled. "I know it's last minute. But they really need our help as fast as possible. I'm sure we can get it together in time. Great, wonderful. I'll check in with you later." She hung up the phone, then snapped her fingers. "Just like that."

"Just like that, what?" Nikki stared at her with wide eyes.

"We're going to have an auction at the country club on Sunday, all of the wealthiest people in Dahlia, and probably some from neighboring cities, will be there." Sonia crossed her arms and smiled. "Pretty impressive, hmm?"

"That's an understatement!" Nikki laughed. "Wow, this is amazing. I can't wait to tell Petra, she's going to be so excited."

"Oh yes, and do ask her to choose a few cute animals to have there at the party. People just love to see what their money is going to support. The cuter they are, the bigger the checks." Sonia winked.

"I can't thank you enough for this, Sonia." Nikki wrapped her arm around her shoulders and pulled her in for a light hug. "You are amazing!"

"Just promise me that next time something is on your mind, you'll tell me." Sonia looked into her eyes. "We're friends, right?"

"Right." Nikki smiled as she turned her attention back to Princess. "I guess I just thought I could solve it myself."

"It never hurts to have a little help." Sonia whistled at Princess as she headed straight for a nearby mailbox. "Not on Mrs. Pennyworth's mailbox, not a chance. She'll have us kicked out of Dahlia in no time."

"If there's anything I can do to help with the party, just let me know." Nikki steered Princess away from the mailbox. "I'm happy to help."

"If you can get there early on Sunday, I'll introduce you to a few people. Plus, it never hurts to have an extra set of hands when throwing a last-minute party. Things can get pretty chaotic, pretty fast." Sonia glanced at her watch. "In fact, I'd better start making some phone calls. Why don't you go fill Petra in about the party? I can walk Princess home."

"Are you sure." Nikki met her eyes with a faint frown.

"Nikki, I've told you to stop looking at me as if I'm an old lady, remember?" Sonia narrowed her eyes, then took the leash from Nikki's hand. "I can handle one little Chihuahua."

"I'm sure you can." Nikki grinned as Princess bolted for the next mailbox.

"Stop right there, beast!" A shrill shriek emitted from the bushes beside the mailbox just before a man wielding hedge-clippers stepped out. His towering frame and broad shoulders added to his domineering appearance. "Don't you dare let that thing wee on my mailbox!" He waved the hedge clippers through the air. "Mrs. Whitter, I've warned you before!"

"Back off, Jerome!" Sonia scooped Princess up into her arms. "Don't you wave those things at me. I'll have you in handcuffs before you can blink."

"Now you're threatening me?" Jerome growled, then looked over at Nikki. "Could you please inform Mrs. Whitter that it is against the law for her creature to urinate on my property?"

"Well, actually—" Nikki began.

"Don't you speak to her. If you have a problem with me, Jerome, then you deal with me." Sonia lifted a thin eyebrow as she met his eyes. "Or perhaps I should just call Mr. Barclay and discuss this incident with him. He might want to know that his accountant is threatening his friends and their innocent canines during his off hours."

"Now you really are threatening me." Jerome sighed as he let the hedge-clippers rest against the side of his leg. "I don't want any trouble, Mrs. Whitter. I just want a wee-free mailbox. Is that so much to ask?"

"Princess would never wee on faux wood." Sonia sniffed as she looked away from the mailbox. "She prefers real oak, as do most with any taste."

"Just keep her away from it." Jerome waved his hand and grunted. "I am going on vacation this weekend, make sure you keep her away from my garden when I'm not here." He pointed his finger at her then turned back to the bush.

Nikki had to hold back a laugh as Sonia met her eyes.

"See? I can handle things just fine." Sonia gave Princess a peck on her furry cheek. "Now, go tell Petra the news. We have lots to do before Sunday."

Nikki smiled as she watched the pair walk off. However, she didn't walk away until she was sure they were far from Jerome. She turned and took a few steps down the street. All of a sudden, she felt water hit her face. She gasped and jumped back.

"Sorry!" A deep voice called out.

"That's okay." Nikki laughed.

"I didn't see you." The man held the garden hose in his hand.

"No problem, Geoff. It's just a bit of water." Nikki smiled, as she wiped some water from her face.

"Mrs. Whitter isn't with you today?" Although

13

short in stature, and slim, the man's sharp features conveyed a sense of authority.

"She was, I just have to rush home to do something." Nikki waved, before she broke into a jog in the direction of her apartment. She couldn't wait to tell Petra that the animal shelter might be saved after all.

CHAPTER 2

The next two days Nikki spent taking phone calls from Sonia and helping out at the shelter as much as she could. On the morning of the fundraiser, her alarm went off an hour earlier than usual. She needed to walk her dogs and stop by the shelter to see if they needed any help getting the two dogs Petra had chosen to attend the fundraiser, ready for their big debut.

Nikki's heart pounded with excitement as she hurried to get ready. It was hard for her to believe that anything could be thrown together so quickly, but she was eager to see what kind of turnout the fundraiser would have.

Nikki tugged on her shoes and headed out the

door. Her cell phone rang before she even picked up the first dog.

"Hi Sonia." Nikki smiled as she heard her friend's voice. "How are things this morning?"

"Coming together. Really." Sonia laughed, and then cleared her throat. "I've got quite a to-do list. Top on it was to touch base with you. I'm bringing Princess with me to the country club, so you won't need to walk her this morning. Also, please try to get there early, because there are so many people I want you to meet."

"I'll do my best." Nikki quickened her pace in the direction of Coco's house. "Do you need me to pick up anything?"

"No, everything is under control, I think. I guess we'll find out. Luckily, most of the donors were already going to be at the country club today. They recently opened a shooting range and today is the grand opening. I think there is going to be a huge turnout. After they're finished at the shooting range, they can bid on some great things, especially from Daniel Barclay's collection. He's offering up so many great items for auction. He's a world traveler and has collected so much over the years. I can't wait to see the response we will get." Sonia gasped.

"Oh dear, is that the right time? Okay, I have to go. See you soon, Nikki."

"See you soon, Sonia." Nikki laughed as she hung up the phone. She was glad to hear Sonia so excited, it gave her a buzz of excitement as well.

After Nikki finished walking the dogs, she returned to her apartment, and picked up her car. On her way to the animal shelter she spotted a familiar car on the road beside her.

Detective Quinn Grant gave a quick honk of his horn and waved to her through the driver's side window of a Dahlia PD patrol car.

"Are you on patrol today?" Since there was no one else on the road, Nikki slowed her car alongside his.

"Yes, pounding the pavement." Quinn grinned as he pointed to his uniform. "What do you think?"

"I could get used to it." Nikki winked at him.

"Don't." Quinn tugged at the collar. "I think I put on some weight since I last wore it."

"You look amazing." Nikki gazed at him for a long moment, then jumped at the sound of a horn.

"Better get moving, or I'm going to have to pull you over." Quinn chuckled as he drove off.

Embarrassed, Nikki stepped on the gas. The person behind her sped up right behind her.

Nikki looked in the rearview mirror and noticed the car was a sleek, bright blue coupe. It didn't look familiar to her, and neither did the man in the driver's seat, who seemed more than eager to let her know how irritated he was.

Nikki sped up a little more but didn't like to go above the speed limit, especially as people often walked, and rode bikes in the area. Despite the fact that she sped up, the car behind her remained right on her tail. Annoyed, she turned on her signal and turned off the main road to take the back way to the animal shelter.

The blue coupe sped past, far beyond the speed limit.

"There's never a cop around when you need one." Nikki rolled her eyes, then laughed at herself.

Nikki pulled into the parking lot of the animal shelter, just as Petra closed the back door on her station wagon.

"Morning Petra." Nikki called out to her through her window. "Do you need any help?"

"No, I think we're all set. I have Bassie in her carrier, and Spots is sprawled out on the back seat. Thanks though. I thought it would be cute to choose a Corgi for an event at the Corgi Country Club."

Petra walked over to Nikki's car. "Are you heading over?"

"Yes, Sonia asked me to get there early. I'm glad you picked Spots and Bassie, I'm sure they will get a lot of attention."

Petra took a deep breath.

"I hope so. My fingers are crossed." She held up her hands to show Nikki. "And my toes, and everything else." She grinned.

"I'm sure it will be great." Nikki waved to her. "I'll see you there."

As Nikki turned back onto the road, she kept an eye out for the blue coupe. Luckily, she didn't see it anywhere. She guessed that it had just blown through the town to the next one. After a few minutes she turned down the long driveway that led to the country club. When she saw the sign for the Corgi Country Club it always brought a smile to Nikki's lips. The country club had been built by a very wealthy family who owned a lot of land in Dahlia. They had named it after their greatest love, Corgis. Their children had inherited their assets, and their love for Corgis, so the name stuck.

Nikki hadn't been to the country club very often. As a child, her family didn't have anything to do with the country club, and as an adult she hadn't had any reason to be there. However, she'd joined Sonia there for lunch a few times over the past year. It always felt a little strange to her, as if it was an entire world unto itself. While the city of Dahlia swirled all around it, the country club with all its vast grounds, luxury and quiet, felt like an island.

Today however, it was no island. As she navigated the parking lot it surprised her to see so many spaces taken. More cars pulled in behind her as well. With an hour to go before the auction, she guessed that many more people had yet to arrive. Sonia was right, it was quite a turnout.

Nikki stepped inside the country club and found staff members bustling in all directions. She managed to get a few directions from a passing waitress and found her way to one of the large banquet rooms. Inside, the room was nicely decorated with several tables and chairs, as well as rows of chairs in front of a small stage and podium. A few people milled about. Sonia finished giving instructions to one of the staff members, then caught sight of Nikki.

"Nikki, I'm glad you're here." Sonia waved her over and smiled. "There's someone that I'd like you to meet."

"Wonderful." Nikki smoothed her hair back

away from her face in an attempt to straighten it out. She could feel dampness against her palms. That morning's walk had been a brisk one and with the warmth in the air she'd been left more sweaty than usual. She wished she'd taken a little extra time to freshen up. Now that she saw the way everyone was dressed, her flower-covered sundress left her feeling a little under-dressed. It seemed like a bad time to meet one of Sonia's high-class friends, but Sonia didn't seem to notice.

"Daniel." Sonia's voice softened into a sing-song tone as she approached a man in a black suit who stood close to the stage in the front of the banquet room.

"Sonia." Daniel turned to face her. One hand slipped down the lapel of his suit jacket. "I heard that you might be here." His lips framed by a thin, silver mustache eased into a smile. "Okay, maybe I had hoped that you would be here."

"When I heard that you offered some items from your collection for the auction, I just knew that this would be a success. Thanks to you, I'm sure that the animal shelter will have more than enough funding for the next few years." Sonia smiled. "You have always been so very generous."

"I try." Daniel gazed at her as his lips curved

into a slow smile. "If you see something you like, be sure to bid on it, I'll make sure you're the winner."

"Oh you." Sonia laughed and shook her head. "I'd better check on a few things, but please keep Nikki in mind if anyone you know needs a dog walker, she is amazing with animals."

"Perhaps she could help that poor woman out then." Daniel clucked his tongue as he looked towards the door.

Nikki turned to see Petra with both dogs on leashes heading in opposite directions.

"Come back." Petra huffed at Bassie who was quite curious about the buffet table. As she tugged Bassie close, Spots tried to weave his way between two chairs. His leash nearly knocked them both over. "Spots!" She groaned while she untangled him, Bassie inched her way towards the food. She almost made it to the edge of the table, when Petra gave her leash a firm tug. "Sit! Both of you just sit!"

"Oh no." Nikki rushed over to Petra and tried to hold in a laugh as she took Bassie's leash from her. "I think they're a little excited."

"You could say that." Petra rolled her eyes as she patted Spots' head. "I'm not sure this one is going to settle down."

"Let me take him for a quick run, that should

help. You can walk Bassie around, she's so friendly." Nikki traded leashes with Petra. "We'll be back soon."

"Thanks, Nikki." Petra flashed a smile at her. "You are a lifesaver, as usual."

Nikki shrugged. "I don't mind at all. I feel far more at home with my four-legged friends than I do with the members of this country club."

"I hear you there." Petra smoothed down her skirt. "I'll see what Sonia needs me to do." She walked over to Sonia with Bassie in tow.

Nikki led Spots outside for a run. As she guided him along the driveway towards the open grass, a man who she didn't recognize rushed past her with his phone pressed to his ear.

"I've told you already, I'll have the money soon, you just have to be patient." He frowned as a truck pulled up in front of him.

"Miller, where do you want the rest of the stuff?" The driver of the truck leaned out the window and waved a well-worn hand at Miller. "Hello? If I don't get this stuff inside soon, the boss is going to fire me."

"Just take it all in." Miller huffed. "I'll be right there." He continued past the truck towards the front door of the country club. "Just a little more time," he muttered into his phone, and then he shoved his phone into his pocket.

Nikki did her best to ignore the tension. It wasn't her business why Miller needed more time, or why the truck driver glared at Miller as if he'd like to murder him. Her business was Spots, and his need for some exercise.

The hyper, happy dog was distracted by every flower and butterfly on the vast grounds of the country club. He wanted to sniff, and pounce on everything he saw. Nikki held him back as he tried to hunt down a squirrel.

"All right, buddy, time to go show you off." Nikki guided him back towards the entrance of the country club. As she neared it, she noticed a familiar car in the parking lot. It was easy to spot, not just because of its bright blue color, but because it wasn't parked in a parking spot. Instead it was parked in the middle of the parking lot. Nikki rolled her eyes at the sight of it. He could have handed his keys over to the valet and the valet would have parked it for him, instead he had blocked several other cars in. She did her best to push the thought from her mind. The day had the potential to be great, and she wanted to do everything to encourage that.

By the time Nikki managed to drag Spots back

into the banquet room, the auction had already started. She walked Spots over to Petra.

"I think he's a little calmer now." Nikki smiled.

"Thanks so much, Nikki. This auction is amazing, the prices just keep going up." Petra grinned.

"Enjoy." Nikki winked at her as a waitress brought over some glasses of wine.

Nikki declined a glass, then looked for Sonia and Princess. After a few minutes she spotted Sonia and Daniel close to the stage, and close to each other. She couldn't help but notice the way Daniel stood right next to Sonia with his arm around her waist. Princess appeared preoccupied with a shiny spot on the floor that kept moving around. Each time it shifted, Princess slapped a paw down on it. Nikki had to hold back her laughter as she watched. Sometimes she believed Princess might just be a cat trapped in a dog's body.

"Up next for auction we have this divine eighteenth century crystal vase. Now, I've been told this needs to be kept quiet, but I think I can trust all of you. Can't I?" Gloria smiled as she leaned across the podium towards the audience. "We're all friends here, after all."

A murmur carried through the crowd that

inspired a smile on Nikki's face. Yes, they all wanted to know the secret of the vase, and hopefully it would make them willing to pay a lot for it.

"The story, as it was shared with me, is that this is a one of a kind handmade vase. It was given as a wedding gift to the artist Pableski. It resided within her house for quite some time." Gloria looked over at the vase and shook her head. "Can you imagine the conversations it might have overheard? Let's start the bidding at three thousand." She smiled as several paddles shot up into the air. As the bidding heated up, the price tag increased. Nikki found herself caught up in the war, as she looked from bidder to bidder to see who would up the offer next. Finally, the price settled on fifteen thousand.

"Going once, going twice, and sold!" Gloria slammed the gavel down onto the podium and let out a squeal of celebration.

Gloria's squeal of celebration turned into a shriek, as Daniel Barclay collapsed to his knees at the front of the crowd. His right hand reached out towards the stage, then he slumped forward. Gasps and murmurs filtered through the crowd as everyone attempted to understand what had happened. Nikki's heart slammed against her chest. All she knew for certain was that something terrible had happened, and she wanted to get to Sonia, to offer her as much support as she could.

"What's wrong?" Nikki frowned as she hurried forward along with a few other people. "Is he having a heart attack?"

"No." Sonia crouched down beside him. Her eyes widened. "He's been shot!"

"Shot?" Nikki took a sharp breath. "How is that possible? I didn't hear a gunshot. I'm sure an ambulance is on its way. I heard Gloria call for one."

Sonia shivered, then gazed down at Daniel.

"It's too late, Nikki." Sonia tightened her grasp on his hand as she shook her head. "He's already gone."

Nikki's breath caught in her throat as she realized that Sonia was right. Daniel was dead!

CHAPTER 3

Two security guards rushed into the room and went straight for Daniel. After they had checked for a pulse, it was obvious that they reached the same conclusion that Nikki and Sonia had.

"Please move towards the exits!" One of the guards gestured towards the exit.

"You need to clear this area now, please." The other guard gestured to Sonia and Nikki. Sonia didn't respond.

"Sonia." Nikki wrapped her arm around her friend's shoulders and tugged her gently away from Daniel. "We need to get out of here."

"Okay." Sonia gave in to Nikki's tugging.

Nikki guided them both through a side door and down a hallway that led to the kitchen.

Sonia suddenly stopped.

"Wait, where's Princess?" She gasped as she swept her gaze around the kitchen. "She was right next to me before Daniel was shot. She must have run off somewhere. Oh no. I was so distracted, I didn't even think to look for her! How could I leave her in there all alone?" She lunged towards the door.

"It's okay." Nikki stepped in front of her. "You stay here, right here. Sit on that chair." She pointed to a stool at the counter behind Sonia. "I'll go get her."

"Nikki, I can come with." Sonia bit into her bottom lip but she swayed slightly.

"Just sit." Nikki guided Sonia into the chair. "I'll just grab Princess, and we'll all be on our way. Will you stay here please?" She looked into Sonia's eyes.

"Yes, I will." Sonia sat down. Her hands fluttered nervously in her lap.

"I won't be long." Nikki pushed open the door to the kitchen. She looked down the short hallway that led back to the banquet room. It was obvious that Daniel had been targeted. She wanted to have another look around the banquet room to see if there were any clues as to who pulled the trigger and why, but her priority was to get Princess. She couldn't leave without Sonia's beloved pet.

Nikki quickly walked towards the door that opened into the banquet room. She heard shouts in the distance. Commands echoed between police officers.

Nikki nudged the door open and peeked through the small space she created. She couldn't see anyone else in the room. Daniel's body remained near the stage. As she searched the room for any sign of Princess, she didn't notice anyone else. Everyone had cleared out, everyone but one Chihuahua.

"Princess!" Nikki clapped her hands together and nudged the door open farther. "Princess, come here!" She clapped her hands again. The sound echoed through the mostly empty, large room. She pushed the door halfway open and put one foot inside the banquet room. "Princess! Come here!" She clapped her hands again.

Sudden pressure against her back, and a strong grip on her arm as it twisted behind her back were the only warnings she received before her body slammed against the wall of the banquet room. She sucked in a breath in the same moment that she attempted to scream. The result was a strangled sound that made her head spin.

"Against the wall! Be still!"

Some relief washed over Nikki as she heard the familiar voice of one of the local Dahlia police officers. At least it wasn't the murderer. At least, she didn't think it was.

"I'm sorry, I'm not armed, I didn't do anything!" Nikki tried to sound calm, but her heart pounded so hard that it was hard to speak clearly.

"Everyone else has vacated the area, and you're sneaking in?" The officer snapped handcuffs closed on her wrists. "Would you like to explain that?" He turned her around to face him in the same moment that Princess bounded towards her, yapping loudly.

"Princess!" Nikki blinked back tears of relief. "Please, Officer, that's my friend's dog. That's why I came back, she got left behind in all of the chaos."

Princess jumped up against Nikki's shins and tried to get behind her to lick her fingertips.

"I see." The officer frowned as he looked down at the dog.

"What is going on here?" Quinn walked into the banquet room, followed by a few more officers. His eyes locked to Nikki's, then dropped to the handcuffs on her wrists. "Get those off her right now."

"It's okay, Quinn." Nikki did her best to keep her voice steady. "It's my fault, I walked in on the scene. I needed to get Princess." She closed her eyes as the officer unlocked the handcuffs. "Thank you." She scooped Princess up into her arms. The dog scrambled up her chest to lick her lips and cheeks. "I know, baby, I know." She hugged Princess gently against her chest.

"Nikki, are you okay?" Quinn traced his fingertips along the curve of her wrist, then looked up to meet her eyes.

"I'm fine." Nikki looked towards Daniel's body. "You have work to do, Quinn. Princess and I are fine."

"Sonia's okay as well?" Quinn frowned as he glanced over at the body.

"Yes, she is. She's in the kitchen waiting for me to get Princess. Have you caught the murderer?" Nikki met his eyes as he turned back to her.

"No, not yet. It looks like a targeted attack." Quinn tipped his head towards the door that led to the hallway. "Go back to Sonia, the lobby has been staged as a space for witnesses to wait."

"Okay." Nikki took a deep breath and turned towards the door.

"Nikki, I'll catch up with you later." Quinn called out to her just before she opened the door.

"Okay." Nikki glanced back and met his eyes briefly, then continued into the hallway.

When Nikki reached the kitchen, Sonia met her at the door.

"Oh, my baby!" Sonia gasped and plucked Princess out of Nikki's arms. "I'm so sorry?" She fluttered light kisses all over the dog's small face. "Can you ever forgive me?"

"She seems to be just fine." Nikki smiled as Princess returned the kisses all over Sonia's face. "Quinn is here now. He said we should go to the lobby."

"Did they catch the terrible person that did this?" Sonia kept Princess in her arms as she led the way through the kitchen.

"Unfortunately no, not yet. But I'm sure it's just a matter of time." Nikki followed her out into the lobby of the country club. It was packed both with the people from the fundraiser, as well as all of the staff of the country club, and several other people that may have been attending other events.

Nikki took a deep breath and did her best to

remain calm. She knew that in times like this panic could spread through a crowd and cause a difficult situation to become worse in a split second. She planned to do her best to avoid that.

"Let's keep to ourselves." Nikki swept her gaze over the crowd. "I'm sure everyone is a little high strung right now."

"A little high strung?" Sonia clutched the necklace that hung against the collar of her mustard yellow dress. "I can't even think straight. I'm more than high strung." She looked back towards the entrance of the lobby. "I keep thinking he might come walking out of there just fine. I keep doubting whether he's really gone."

"I'm sorry, Sonia." Nikki hugged her. "I got so caught up in everything, I forgot, you've lost a friend."

"Not a friend exactly." Sonia met her eyes, and opened her mouth to say more, but she was interrupted by another voice.

"Nikki." Quinn called out to her. "I need to speak to you."

"Excuse me a minute, Sonia." Nikki gave her shoulder a squeeze, then walked over to Quinn.

Nikki glanced back over her shoulder at Sonia, then met Quinn's eyes.

"I don't want to leave her for too long. This has been quite a shock for her."

"I'm sure it has." Quinn frowned as he looked over at Sonia. "A few people have mentioned that she was standing right beside the victim when he was shot. Did she tell you who pulled the trigger?"

"No. I mean, yes, she was standing right beside him, but she didn't see anything. She didn't see who shot Daniel."

"Are you sure about that?" Quinn narrowed his eyes as he looked back at her. "She was right there."

"I know she was. I wasn't far away, either." Nikki shook her head. "She didn't see anything."

"That banquet room was packed full of people, and everyone we have spoken to so far claims they didn't see anything." Quinn's jaw rippled with tension as he lowered his voice. "How is that possible?"

"I was there." Nikki crossed her arms as she leaned back against the wall. "I know how a room full of people didn't witness anything, because I was one of them. None of us even knew what happened at first. The gavel struck the podium and muffled the sound of a gunshot. That's the only thing I can think of that makes sense. That, or whoever pulled the trigger had a silencer on the gun. But either way, from what I've heard no one has any idea who did it. Do they?"

"No, but one person who was there, knows." Quinn leaned closer to her and guided her closer to the wall of the lobby as his eyes locked to hers. "Nikki, someone in that room pointed a gun at Daniel and pulled the trigger. The killer did this with people all around. This was a targeted attack. You may not think that you saw anything, but you did."

"Whether I did or not, what does it matter?" Nikki shifted away from him along the wall and closed her eyes. "I'm sorry. I don't want to disappoint you, but I don't remember anything out of the ordinary."

"It's okay." Quinn placed his palms lightly on her shoulders. "Nikki, I'm not trying to pressure you. What happened in that banquet room, it was nothing that anyone expected. Something may come to you, and when it does, I hope that you will share it with me."

"Of course, I will." Nikki felt some comfort from the warmth of his touch, but her muscles still tensed. She was there, she should know exactly what happened, and yet the only thing that echoed through her mind was the sound of the gavel as it struck the podium. The same people that had milled around her in the banquet room, now surrounded her in the lobby. She only knew a few of the faces, she had no idea if there was a face missing from the crowd. As she walked back over to Sonia, she felt the pressure of many eyes looking in her direction.

"You okay, Sonia?" Nikki took her hand.

"I feel like everyone's staring at me." Sonia wiped at her eyes with a tissue clutched tightly in her slender fingers.

"I think they might be," Nikki whispered as she stepped closer to Sonia. "You were right beside Daniel when he was killed. I think people might assume that you know who killed him."

"But I don't." Sonia pursed her lips. "I didn't see anything at all."

"I know that." Nikki sighed. "I didn't see anything either. I keep asking myself, what did I miss? What did I see that I can't recall?"

"Just take a breath, Nikki." Sonia rubbed her palm along Nikki's forearm. "Once the shock fades, we might remember a thing or two, but that certainly won't happen while we're stuck here."

"I'm going to find an officer who is free. Maybe if we give our statements about what happened we can get out of here." Nikki looked through the sea of officers that populated the lobby. Many of them were from Dahlia, but others were from cities outside of Dahlia. She guessed that Dahlia PD had called in assistance. When she spotted an officer walking away from one of the country club's staff members, she took Sonia's hand and pulled her over to him. "Sir, what will it take for us to be able to leave?" Nikki did her best to keep her voice calm and quiet.

"Can I please have your name, address and phone number? And see some identification?" After Nikki and Sonia gave their details, he looked up at them. "Come over here please." He led them over to a table where a female officer stood, with gloves on. "Hold out your hands." The officer tucked his clipboard under his arm. "We're checking everyone for gunshot residue."

"Oh, clever." Sonia nodded as she held out one hand. She continued to hold onto Princess with the other arm.

"It's part of the process." The male officer nodded as the female officer began to swab her hand. "Can you give a description of the murderer?"

"No, sir. I'm sorry." Sonia glanced at Nikki.

"Neither can I. Neither of us saw who pulled the

trigger." Nikki frowned as she took Princess from Sonia.

Sonia held out her other hand.

"Everything was normal, and then it wasn't."

"I understand." The male officer glanced up at her. "Did you overhear anyone exchanging words? Maybe someone who wasn't happy about the bidding?"

"No, not at all." Sonia sighed. "Everyone seemed to be having a great time. The fundraiser was quite a success."

"And, the victim, Daniel Barclay, did you know him?" The male officer looked straight into her eyes.

"Sure, I knew him. We'd known each other for quite some time." Sonia cleared her throat as the officer turned his attention to Nikki.

"How well?" The male officer asked.

The female officer waited while Nikki handed Princess to Sonia, then held out her hands to her.

"Oh, not too well. We ran in the same social circle. We had mutual friends." Sonia shrugged. "I'm sorry I'm not much help."

"You'd be surprised what can be helpful." He took notes as the female officer swabbed Nikki's hands. He turned to Nikki. "Any little thing that you can remember might make a difference. Did you know the victim?"

"Not at all. I'd just met him for the first time today." Nikki watched as he made another note on his clipboard. "Are we free to go now?"

"Yes. Here's my card." He handed her a business card. "Please, if you think of anything, feel free to contact me, or Dahlia PD." He paused as he looked at her again. "Oh wait. Nikki, you can always contact Quinn. He's the detective in charge of the investigation." The officer winked at her, then turned and walked away.

"Well, that was a little unprofessional." Sonia pursed her lips.

"It was." Nikki frowned, then couldn't help but smile a little. "But it probably means that Quinn has been talking about me, doesn't it?"

"It sure does." Sonia looped her arm through Nikki's. "Would you mind driving me and Princess home, Nikki? Gloria picked us up, so I don't have my car here."

"Of course, I'll drive you home." Nikki pushed thoughts of Quinn from her mind as she focused on her friend.

41

CHAPTER 4

*I*n the parking lot of the country club where there were still many cars parked, Nikki looked for one in particular, a blue coupe. It was no longer parked in the middle of the parking lot. Did that mean the driver had moved it, or had he already left?

Nikki pulled open the passenger side door on her car, and once Sonia and Princess were settled, she walked around to the driver's side. After a quick glance back at the country club, she climbed in and turned the key in the ignition. The car coughed but wouldn't start. Nikki sighed as she turned the key again. It was getting more difficult to start and she had finally relented and booked it in with the mechanic the following day. She knew if she didn't get it looked at, it was just a matter of time before it would get stuck. She couldn't afford a new car. She just hoped that it lasted until tomorrow. On the fourth try the car sputtered to life and Nikki sighed with relief.

The drive to Sonia's house was quick and quiet. Nikki searched her mind for the one right thing to say, but nothing felt appropriate. Sonia had lost a friend, more than that, he had been assassinated, as he stood right beside her. What could she say that would make that easier?

"Do you mind if I stay with you for a bit?" Nikki parked close to the front door of Sonia's house.

"I'd love that, thank you." Sonia and Princess headed for the door while Nikki took a moment to check her phone. Nothing from Quinn. Of course not, he was busy investigating the case. He wouldn't have a moment to spare, and she understood that. But she kept hoping that he would send her a quick text to tell her that the killer had been captured. Would she find out from him, or the local news?

As Nikki stepped into Sonia's house, she continued to search her memory for anything that might be important to the case.

"Nikki, are you okay?" Sonia set a plate of her favorite peanut butter cookies down on the dining room table in front of her, as Nikki sat down in a chair.

"Me?" Nikki blinked and focused on her friend, instead of the thoughts that had been running through her mind. "I'm the one that should be asking you that."

"I'm fine." Sonia plucked a cookie from the plate and sat down across from her. "Not fine, no." She sighed, then nibbled at the edge of the cookie. "What happened was terrible, and I can't get it out of my mind. I need to do something. I need to find out who killed Daniel. I can't stop thinking about it."

"Of course, you want to know what happened." Nikki placed her hand over Sonia's and met her eyes. "I know that you cared about him."

"Sure, I cared about him. But we weren't close. I wouldn't really even consider us friends, more like acquaintances."

"He seemed pretty friendly when he had his arm around you." Nikki quirked a brow as she gazed at her friend. Sonia could be private about things, but as their friendship had progressed, she'd shared quite a bit with Nikki. At that moment though, she sensed some hesitation.

"He was always a flirt." Sonia laughed and

waved her hand. "He would put his arm around any woman that was nearby. It was nothing, trust me." She sank down in her chair and closed her eyes. "The thing about Daniel is, he was always on the prowl. Not just with women either, but with business. He could suss out a good investment in the blink of an eye, and once he did, he would do everything in his power to make it his."

"It sounds like he was a little ferocious." Nikki broke off a small piece of her cookie and offered it to Princess, who happily ate it. Sonia kept Princess on a very strict diet but had recently started allowing her to have a treat at the table now and then. Nikki presumed it was because it made Princess so happy.

"He was. He could make you feel like the most unique and wonderful person on the planet one minute, and the next he would destroy you. I wouldn't say he was normal in that way." Sonia tipped her head to the side. "I always wondered if he might have a bit of a personality disorder."

"He sounds like an interesting man, who may have had quite a few enemies." Nikki took a bite of her cookie, then looked across the table at Sonia. "Do you know of any in particular?"

"We hadn't been in touch recently. Not really,

anyway. I'd heard a few things about him, but I never really paid attention to his business dealings. As far as enemies, I'm sure he had more than a few." Sonia narrowed her eyes. "Like I said, once you became his target, he would stop at nothing to either get what he wanted or destroy you."

"Sounds a little frightening." Nikki set her cookie down and met Sonia's eyes. "Did he do something like that to you?"

"Me?" Sonia laughed and clutched at the necklace that hung around her neck. "No, of course not."

"It's getting late. I really have to get the dogs out for their afternoon walk. Are you going to be okay here by yourself, Sonia?" Nikki stood up from the table.

"I won't be by myself. Princess will be with me. I think she's had enough excitement for today." Sonia yawned, then shook her head. "I think we could both use a rest."

"All right, but if you need anything, let me know." Nikki walked around the table and put her arm around Sonia. "I'm sorry for your loss."

"Thank you, Nikki." Sonia patted her arm, then smiled up at her.

Nikki searched her eyes for a moment as she

sensed that Sonia might want to say something more. Instead, Sonia turned her attention back to her cookie.

As Nikki walked out of the house, she fought the urge to go back, and try to get more information from Sonia. Why was she holding something back? It wasn't like her. Nikki sighed as she started her car. Maybe she was just being paranoid. She wondered about Petra and the dogs. Had they made it back to the shelter okay? She decided she would check on them after she had taken the dogs out for their walk.

Nikki dropped her car off at her apartment, then started on her journey to collect the dogs. With each leash she clipped on, she felt some comfort. It wasn't just the routine of completing her job that made her feel calmer, it was the eager licks, the happy barks, and the incessant tail wagging.

One thing Nikki had found over the years of running her dog-walking business, it was nearly impossible not to smile when the dogs greeted her. No matter what mood she was in at the beginning of the walk, by the end, her spirits had been lifted, and her perspective had changed. She counted on that psychological boost today as she steered the dogs towards the park, that had been nicknamed Pooch

Park by the locals because it was a favorite for them to take their dogs.

Nikki took deep breaths of the fragrant air as she bounded with them along the path that wound through the thick, green grass and towering trees that filled the park. It was a place of peace, and exactly what she needed. However, even as she laughed at the dogs' joint attempts to terrorize a squirrel, her mind flashed back to those final moments at the country club. Quinn insisted that she, or someone in the banquet room must have seen the murderer. She realized that it was most likely her that would have seen the murderer. She had stepped in from the back of the room, she had walked forward through the crowd. She had likely laid her eyes on the murderer as he or she escaped or blended in with the group of people. Why couldn't she remember seeing anything strange? Could someone really murder another person, and then seem perfectly normal?

As Nikki and the dogs rounded the bend towards the exit of the park, it was as if the dogs began to compete to see who could get their leash the most tangled up.

Nikki took a moment to straighten them out. As she sorted through the leashes, she recalled Spots' nervous energy. He couldn't settle down. Was that because he was a hyper dog, or had he already sensed that something was wrong? She knew that dogs were great readers of personalities, and intentions. Maybe Spots had been trying to tell her something. She recalled the man who walked past her, barking into his phone. Spots hadn't liked him. But then again, she hadn't liked him too much herself. She didn't want to jump to any false conclusions.

As Nikki left the park behind and began dropping dogs off at their homes, she felt determination grow within her. She couldn't just wait to see how things turned out. She needed to know the truth about what happened to Daniel, as much for herself, as for Sonia.

With just Coco left to take home, Nikki slowed her pace. She wanted to savor the peace of his company for as long as she could. However, as she neared his house, Coco began to tug at his leash. She tightened her grip on the leash. Coco's strength could be a force to be reckoned with at times. He tugged again, she stumbled forward a few steps.

"Coco, relax." Nikki frowned, then crouched down to pet him. "We're almost home, buddy.

What's up? Are you hungry?" She scratched behind his ear.

Coco looked into her eyes, then whimpered.

"Okay, hon." Nikki stood up, unnerved by his behavior and eager to give him the comfort of home. She quickened her pace towards his street. As Nikki walked, she searched for anything that might be the source of his restlessness. Sometimes the local cats drew his attention. Sometimes it was one of the local kids teasing him. No one walked down the street, no kids peeked through fences, no cats were in his path. She did detect a smoky scent in the air. Perhaps someone's cook-out had stirred up Coco's appetite. He did like to eat. Again, maybe her own paranoia had triggered suspicion, when there was nothing at all to be suspicious about.

CHAPTER 5

Coco began to bark as Nikki neared his house. She glanced around, curious as to what he might have seen. Coco did like to bark. But he usually only did it when something caught him off guard. It could be anything from a leaf on the loose, to a squirrel bolting up a nearby tree. His barking increased the closer they got to his house. The street was empty, but for some birds perched in the trees. The trees blew in the breeze, but nothing sounded out of place.

"What is it, buddy?" Nikki narrowed her eyes. "Is something wrong?"

Coco pulled on his leash as he stepped onto his driveway. He barked louder and gave a faint snarl.

Nikki caught sight of a shadow along the front of Coco's house.

"Nikki?" A familiar voice called out, before a man stepped off Coco's porch.

"Quinn." Nikki breathed a sigh of relief as she smiled. "What are you doing here?"

"Sorry, I didn't mean to startle you, or you, Coco." Quinn reached into his pocket and pulled something out of it. Then he crouched down and opened his hand to Coco.

Coco gave one last bark, then snatched the treat out of Quinn's palm. He wagged his tail and gave Quinn's hand a quick lick of gratitude.

"Ugh, thanks for that." Quinn cringed and pulled a tissue out of his other pocket. As he wiped his hand off, he met Nikki's eyes. "I've been waiting for you."

"You have?" Nikki guided Coco towards the door of the house. "Is it about Daniel? Give me a second, let me just get him settled."

"Sure, of course." Quinn leaned back against the railing of the porch.

Nikki made sure that Coco's water dish was full, then locked the door behind her as she stepped back out onto the porch. She caught sight of Quinn as the sunlight played across his hair and face. For just a second, her breath caught in her throat. Quinn, the boy two years older than her who she'd had a crush on since high school, was now a man, and a detective. Since he'd moved back to Dahlia, they'd reconnected, and as they tentatively navigated a new relationship, she still felt a little starstruck when he smiled at her.

"Did you figure out who did it?" Nikki walked over to lean against the railing beside him.

"Far from it I'm afraid. We have numerous suspects, and none that I like." Quinn folded his arms across his chest and sighed. "Actually, the reason I'm here, is because I'd like your input on Mrs. Whitter."

"Sonia?" Nikki looked over at him. "What kind of input?"

"I know that she has known Daniel for many years, there is a lot of history there, and so far it seems there weren't too many people who were close to him." Quinn met her eyes. "Has she mentioned anything to you about who she might suspect?"

"They weren't as close as you think." Nikki shook her head. "She told me they were friends, but not very friendly, more like acquaintances."

"Ah, I see." Quinn nodded.

"What is it?" Nikki stepped in front of him and tried to meet his eyes. "What aren't you telling me?"

"My investigation has revealed that Sonia's late husband, James Whitter, and Daniel Barclay were in business together many years ago. Apparently, they had a huge falling out." Quinn leaned back against the railing.

"Really?" Nikki's eyes widened.

"She didn't mention anything to you about it?"

"No, I wonder why?" Nikki shook her head. "She must have a reason. She wouldn't keep important information from the police."

"Maybe it's just not something she wanted to talk about. She does seem like a private person." Quinn curled his hands around the railing and shook his head. "It's hard to say. But I'm going to have to dig into it, and I wanted to see if she mentioned anything about it to you."

"No, she didn't." Nikki frowned.

"Maybe it just skipped her mind." Quinn met her eyes and smiled. "You know I care about her as well. I don't want to cause her any trouble. But I do wonder why she hasn't shared this information with the police, and why apparently she hasn't shared it with you, either."

"Like I said, she must have a reason." Nikki

turned away from the railing and stepped down off the porch. "Whatever it is, it's probably best to leave it alone."

Quinn followed her off the porch down onto the driveway, then shoved his hands into his pockets.

"Nikki, I can't do that." Quinn shook his head. "This case has to be fully investigated, and right now the only lead I have is the discrepancy in Mrs. Whitter's statement."

"What are you planning to do?" Nikki stared at him. "Interrogate her? Do you consider her a suspect?"

"No, of course not." Quinn raised an eyebrow.

"Look, like you said, Sonia can be private about some things. I'm sure if she's private about this, then she has a reason."

"I understand that, but this is a murder investigation, Nikki." Quinn put his hands on his hips. "I need to know everything that could be relevant."

"I know, but if she didn't tell you about the business relationship, then I doubt it's relevant." Nikki looked at him. "Why can't you just leave it alone?"

"Can you?" Quinn looked into her eyes as he waited for an answer.

Nikki wanted to insist that she could, but already her mind was filled with curiosity. Why would Sonia hide something like this from her? Why would she keep this from the police?

"Like I said, I have no interest in interrogating her." Quinn closed the distance between them and paused in front of her. "I thought maybe you could talk to her. Encourage her to come forward with what information she might have. I don't want to do anything to upset her, but it's my job to investigate this case. Honestly, if I don't take the right steps quickly, someone else is going to take them for me. At least if you talk to her first, we might be able to avoid all of the unpleasantness."

"Unpleasantness." Nikki nodded slowly. "That's something we definitely want to avoid. Quinn, you know she had nothing to do with this."

"I know, but I have to do something." Quinn frowned. "She hasn't told us all the information that might be relevant, Nikki. That's the only thing I know for certain right now in this case. Am I supposed to just ignore that?"

"No." Nikki sighed.

"So, will you talk to her?" Quinn met her eyes. "Ask her to come talk to me about her connection with Daniel."

"I can try." Nikki looked into his eyes. "But I won't keep anything from her. I am going to be upfront about it. As long as it's okay with Sonia, you can trust me to share any information with you that I think will help you find the murderer."

"That's all I'm asking." Quinn held his hand out to her. "But keep in mind, sometimes the oddest clue can be exactly what solves the case."

"I will." Nikki took his hand and gave it a soft squeeze. "I know that if it was anybody else, you wouldn't be offering this kind of courtesy. I do appreciate that."

"Thanks." Quinn pulled his hand free, then placed a light kiss on her cheek. "I need to get back to the station. Please let me know once you've spoken to her." He rested his hand on her shoulder and gazed into her eyes. "Sooner is better than later."

"I hear you." Nikki nodded, then smiled at him as he turned to walk away.

Nikki knew that she needed to get Sonia to be forthcoming with the information, so there was no reason for the police to suspect or question her. She couldn't imagine the woman being locked in an interrogation room. She just wasn't sure if she was more worried about Quinn or Sonia in that situation. She doubted their relationship would remain the same. She had to keep that from happening.

After finally getting her car to start she drove to Sonia's. Normally, she would walk but she didn't want to spend the time. She wanted to be face to face with Sonia as soon as possible. No matter how she spun Quinn's words she couldn't think of a reasonable explanation for Sonia not telling her everything. What could she have been thinking when she kept it from the police? Didn't she know that the truth would eventually come out?

CHAPTER 6

*N*ikki pulled into the circular driveway in front of Sonia's house and parked the car. As she sat in the silence, she considered the best way to approach the situation. It appeared as if Sonia was hiding something, but Nikki trusted Sonia and she didn't want to alienate her in any way. Nikki stepped out of her car and walked to the front door.

"Nikki, I was wondering why you were sitting out there." Sonia laughed as she opened the door. "Did you forget something earlier?"

"No." Nikki took a deep breath, then met her eyes. "Sonia, I need to talk to you."

"Okay, sure." Sonia stepped aside and opened the door wider.

Princess ran up to the door and yapped happily at Nikki's shins.

"Hi sweetie." Nikki reached down to pet her, then looked up at Sonia.

"What's going on? Is it the shelter? Something about Daniel?" Sonia frowned as she led Nikki into the living room.

"Something about Daniel, yes." Nikki sat down on the couch and waited for Sonia to sit down beside her. "Sonia, I know that you like your privacy."

"I do. Doesn't everyone?" Sonia smiled some, then gave Nikki's shoulder a light shove. "Relax hon, it's just me, not a firing squad. Whatever it is, just spit it out. We can figure it out."

"Quinn came to me this afternoon, and he told me that your late husband and Daniel used to be in business together." Nikki shifted on the couch cushion. "He said they had a falling out."

"Ah." Sonia sat back against the couch and folded her hands in her lap. "He said that, did he?"

"Yes, he did." Nikki studied her. She noticed the way her usually lively eyes settled on one spot and stared. Her rarely still hands, clung to each other. At that moment, her petite frame looked downright tiny, as if she might be swallowed up by the luxurious cushions that surrounded her. "He wants you to come forward with the information. He thinks it looks suspicious that you kept it from the police."

"Oh, I didn't think it was relevant. That's all. It never even occurred to me to mention it. It happened so long ago." Sonia's eyes continued to stare at the vase in the center of the coffee table. "I wonder what happened to Daniel's vase. The one that was up for auction." She squeezed her hands together tighter and looked up at Nikki. "My husband had many business partners over the years. I didn't even think about telling the police about it. I had nothing to do with his business affairs."

"I understand, but I think you need to talk to Quinn about it before it looks suspicious that you kept the information from the police. Quinn has a job to do. He has uncovered evidence that you weren't forthcoming in your statement. Now, he doesn't want to pursue it himself, but he knows that if he doesn't someone else will." Nikki shifted closer to Sonia on the couch.

"I understand, the truth is, James could be very ruthless in business, a lot like Daniel. I tried to keep away from it at all costs. I didn't think that their relationship was relevant to the murder, and I didn't want to rehash the past. I don't really know the details of what happened, anyway. James kept me out of the business, and I preferred it that way."

"I understand." Nikki placed her hand over Sonia's and held her gaze. "Do you know anything about what happened between them?"

"He was in business with my husband many years ago and although there was some bad blood between them at the time, we were still acquainted. They were both very strong willed, and they both wanted to be in charge so they decided to sever their business ties. I did hear from a mutual friend that Daniel swindled James out of some money when he left the business. When I asked James about it, he said that it was better to take the loss than burn more bridges. I imagine that it stung, though. James was a very proud man. James and Daniel shared many mutual friends." Sonia sighed. "Somehow they both managed to keep business separate from their personal lives. If James didn't, I imagine we would have had no friends at all."

"Is there anything else you can tell me about Daniel? Anyone else that could have wanted him dead?" Nikki asked.

"Well yes. Daniel Barclay was not only a ruthless businessman, he was a womanizer." Sonia's lips tightened as she stood up from the couch. "He had a relationship with a couple of friends of mine and left them heartbroken because he couldn't commit."

"So, there was nothing romantic between you two after your husband passed away?" Nikki frowned as she watched her friend hover between the coffee table and the couch.

"No nothing, never." Sonia sat back down on the couch.

"I think he wanted something more from you." Nikki smiled. "I saw the way he looked at you. You may think that you were just an acquaintance, but I suspect that you were a lot more to him than that."

"Maybe." Sonia shrugged. "I guess now, we'll never know." She met Nikki's eyes. "Is that enough to satisfy Quinn?"

"I think he would be curious about whether you discovered anything about Daniel during the time he was in business with your husband, and for the years you knew him. He would want to know any enemies or secrets that might explain what happened to him." Nikki patted the back of Sonia's hand as she studied her. "Anything that you think might lead to his killer."

"If there was something, you know I would have

told the police that. I want his killer found. He might not have been the best man when it came to morals, but he didn't deserve to be killed. He had a long life ahead of him, and he could have done a lot of good during the years that he had left with the fortune that he amassed." Sonia narrowed her eyes. "Now, I don't know where it will go. I suppose it might all go to waste."

"He didn't have any children?" Nikki raised an eyebrow. "I would think with his reputation for playing the field he might have had at least one."

"None that I know of, he was always very adamant that he didn't want to have children. It wasn't that he disliked them, he just didn't like the idea of bringing more people into an overcrowded world." Sonia shook her head. "I'm assuming he had a will. My guess is that he left quite a bit to Jerome, his accountant, they had been friends for so long. But that is just a guess. I imagine he might have left some if not all of his fortune to charity. Hopefully, some good might still come from all of this."

"Hopefully." Nikki nodded and squeezed her hand. "No matter what, we're going to find out what happened to him, Sonia."

"Anything I can do to help, you just let me

know." Sonia looked into her eyes. "I want whoever did this to be caught."

"Me too. But today, you should rest." Nikki stood up and walked towards the door. "Promise me you will?"

"Of course." Sonia smiled. "What else would I do?"

Nikki said goodbye to Princess then closed the door behind her. She left Sonia's house feeling as if a weight had been lifted off her shoulders. Sonia had explained why she had kept the information from the police, and Nikki understood her reasoning. When Nikki reached her apartment, she called Quinn as she stepped inside. After his voicemail picked up, she left him a quick message.

"Quinn, I spoke to Sonia. There really isn't anything she can offer. She didn't mention the business fallout between her husband and Daniel to the police because she didn't think it was relevant. It was so long ago and it was no longer an issue, especially seeing as James has been deceased for quite a few years. She did mention that Daniel was a ruthless businessman, and a bit of a player. He might have angered the wrong woman, but considering all his other enemies, I doubt that is the most likely scenario."

Nikki ended the call, then sprawled out on her couch. As she closed her eyes, her mind filled with thoughts of that day. She'd been looking at the vase as the description was given. She'd seen the reflection of something, a shadowy shape, on the surface of the vase. It could have been anything. But it stuck in her mind. Had she seen more than she realized? She recalled the sound of the dogs barking, and the shock. She'd stood there, stunned, as she processed what had just occurred. She'd watched, as Sonia crouched down beside Daniel, and clung to his hand. Someone had murdered him, and she needed to do something to help find the murderer. She couldn't do nothing.

Nikki grabbed her phone and began to search through any information she could find about Daniel. There were plenty of complaints on the local social media pages about his business behavior, but nothing she could find about any recent romantic connections. Was Daniel single? She began to dig a little deeper into dating websites. If Daniel was a player, she guessed that he hadn't given up the habit of dating who and when he could. She skimmed through a few sites, but it was hard to get any details without signing up.

Nikki returned to his social media profiles and

began to search through the history of his posts. Finally, she came across one that was connected with a particular dating app. She found the app, and selected download. She stared at her screen as the app loaded onto her phone. She hadn't dated much, she'd never joined an online dating service or app. At twenty-four she still liked the idea of meeting people the old-fashioned way. Online profiles and chats felt so sterile and distant to her. But many of her friends had made lasting connections on them.

"All right, Daniel, let's see what you were up to on this app." Nikki began to search it, then cringed as she realized she had to set up an account to view anything. Each step of setting up her profile was more irritating than the last. She had to describe herself, select her interests, choose the type of person she might be interested in meeting, and even give an example of a perfect date. By the time she got through the process, her skin crawled with the strangeness of it. When the site requested a picture, her heart skipped a beat. Did she really want to put a picture of herself on some random dating site?

"It's only for long enough to get information about Daniel." Nikki sighed. Then she smiled to herself as she selected a photograph. She chose her favorite picture on her phone of Princess, and set it as her profile picture. Perhaps the site would reject it, but for the moment it was enough to get her through to the profiles of other members.

Nikki began searching for Daniel. It took her a few minutes to find him as he hadn't created a profile under his name, but under Barclay Smith. "Got yourself into so much trouble you had to go by a different name, huh?" Nikki shook her head as she skimmed through his profile. He boasted about his business successes, his athletic activities, and his favorite sports teams. His profile picture appeared to be dated by about ten years, and his perfect date involved a helicopter and a private beach. "No wonder you got so much attention." Nikki laughed to herself. Then she noticed a star rating beside his name. He had three and a half out of five gold stars. "What does that mean?" She clicked on the stars. Her eyes widened as a list of reviews popped up in front of her. "You've got to be kidding me." She shook her head as she read through some of the reviews. They ranged from 'Player stay away' to 'Gentleman, he spoiled me like I deserve'. However, one review in particular held her attention.

'Daniel, I've tried to reach you many times. You can't keep avoiding me. Please contact me. I just want a chance with you. That's all I'm asking.' Nikki read it over again, then clicked on the name associated with the review. 'Ava Dunn.'

Nikki read over the woman's profile. She listed herself as a thirty-five year old woman, and went on to include her interests. In her hobbies, she included playing tennis at the local country club. "Interesting." She jotted down the name, and other information, including an e-mail address. It seemed like an obsessive thing to post on a dating site, but then she didn't have a lot of experience with using them. As Nikki tried to investigate further, the words on the screen blurred. She blinked, then they blurred again. Then she yawned.

Exhausted, she set her phone down and sprawled out on the couch. Maybe some rest would help loosen up the memories of the day and give her some insight into who the killer might be.

CHAPTER 7

After Nikki left, Sonia tried to relax, but she just couldn't. She needed to do something to help find Daniel's murderer. She thought about calling Nikki to join her, but she knew she was busy and didn't want to bother her. Sonia called Princess over and clipped on her leash.

"Yes, you're ready for a walk aren't you, baby?" She smiled at her.

Princess gazed up at her with wide eyes.

"Don't look at me like that." Sonia clucked her tongue. "I can walk you without Nikki." She led the dog out through the front door, down the long driveway, and along the sidewalk. Princess bounded forward, pleased to be outside. But Sonia's focus remained on a particular neighbor's house. Would he be home? She hoped so. He often worked from home and she knew from experience that he routinely watered his plants twice a day, around the same time, in the morning and evening. As she hoped, she found Geoff in front of his garden, with hose in hand.

"Geoff." Sonia tightened her grip on Princess' leash as she walked across his well-manicured grass to reach him.

"Mrs. Whitter?" Geoff glanced over at her.

"Oh Geoff, I wanted to check on you. You must be heartbroken." Sonia studied his face as he glanced at her again. In his late forties, Geoff actually looked quite a few years younger. He had a babyface that was enhanced by the bright blue eyes that stared at her.

"It's a tragedy." Geoff nodded, then looked back at his flowers. "So unexpected."

"Was it?" Sonia inched a little closer to him. "I mean, did he have any reason to fear for his life?"

"I have no idea." Geoff aimed the hose at the plants and continued to water them. "I wouldn't think so. Although, as you know from personal experience, he had many enemies from his past that might want him dead."

"What?" Sonia took a slight step back. "What do you mean by that?"

"I know he was in business with your husband before he passed. I wasn't his lawyer then, but I was part of his circle, and I remember the way the business partnership ended." Geoff met her eyes. "Have you told the police about that?"

"They know about it, but it has no bearing on what's happened now." Sonia shook her head, annoyed. She cleared her throat as she did her best to calm down the frustration that his comment stirred. Now wasn't the time to dwell on the past, now was the time to catch a killer. She knew the best way to do that was while everyone's knowledge of Daniel was fresh in their minds. "Geoff, you knew him best." Sonia crossed her arms as she looked into the lawyer's eyes when he glanced at her again. "I know that you were friends for a long time. You must be aware of any issues he might have been having with his current investors and business partners."

"That would make sense." Geoff nodded, then turned his attention back to his flower garden. "But unfortunately, we hadn't been as close lately as we used to be." He aimed the hose at the soil beneath the bright yellow daffodils. "The truth is, he'd been acting more secretive. I used to be the only person he trusted, but over the past few weeks, he stopped confiding in me. I tried to get him to talk to me about what was wrong, but he just dismissed me, and claimed that I had nothing to be concerned about." He narrowed his eyes. "I guess he really was hiding something."

"And you never even got a sense of what it might be?" Sonia pointed to his hand that held the hose. "I think you're overdoing it there, Geoff."

"What do you mean?" Geoff jerked his hand away and frowned.

"The flowers." Sonia gestured to the river of water that flooded the soil.

"Oh." Geoff blinked as he turned the hose away from the flowers, then twisted the nozzle to stop the flow. "I'm sorry, I've found it hard to concentrate ever since the auction." He closed his eyes briefly, then opened them again to look at Sonia. "I'm sure it wasn't easy for you either, you were right there with him."

"I was." Sonia nodded.

"And yet, you have no idea who shot him?" Geoff raised an eyebrow as he turned to face her. A few droplets of water slid from the metal ring of the hose and dripped onto Sonia's shoe.

Sonia drew her foot back and frowned.

"I didn't see the murderer, no. If I had, I would have told the police what I saw."

"Shame." Geoff shook his head. "You would have been a perfect eye-witness."

"I was a little distracted. I was looking at the beautiful vase that Daniel had put up for auction, and I just—" Sonia pressed her hand against her chest. "I never would have imagined that someone could be in that banquet room with murderous intentions."

"I'd be surprised if just about everyone in that room didn't harbor some kind of desire to see Daniel dead." Geoff lowered his voice. "Mrs. Whitter, like you said, I've worked for him for a long time. He's crossed many people in that time. He was ruthless when it came to business. He never hesitated to crush someone when he saw the opportunity arise."

"I know that Daniel could be cold, and his work was his number one priority, but I'm sure he didn't do anything that would cause someone to wish death on him." Sonia narrowed her eyes. "What makes you think he did?"

"Maybe all the threats he told me about." Geoff shrugged.

"I thought you said you didn't know much about who might be upset with him?" Sonia studied his expression as he rolled his eyes.

"I said I didn't know much about any recent issues. But over the years, sure I've dealt with a lot of threats against him."

"Did you tell the police about those old threats?" Sonia scooped Princess up into her arms to keep her from traipsing through the mud.

"I'm a lawyer, remember?" Geoff smirked. "I told the police what I had to, and nothing more. Whoever pulled that trigger wasn't some angry business associate. It was someone who had a personal vendetta against Daniel, I guarantee it. As I'm sure you're aware, he didn't exactly leave any hearts intact."

"You think it was a spurned lover?" Sonia's eyes widened.

"I think it's very possible, yes. I warned him more than once about his behavior. I told him that one day, he was going to cross the wrong woman, and she was going to make him pay for his dalliances." Geoff tightened his lips. "He just laughed at me, told me I was jealous. Honestly, Mrs. Whitter." He looked over at her. "I thought the way he treated the women in his life was cruel."

"Had he been seeing someone lately?" Sonia asked.

"Like I said, he'd been secretive. Whatever was going on in his life, I wasn't part of it. Now, if you'll excuse me, I do have an appointment to get to." Geoff coiled the hose back up and hung it on a stand near his front door. As he disappeared inside, Sonia stared after him. If he really thought it was someone that Daniel was dating, then she guessed he wasn't as out of the loop as he claimed. As far as what Geoff knew about his business dealings with James, she couldn't help but wonder what Daniel might have revealed to him.

"It doesn't matter now, Sonia," she said to herself as she walked with Princess in her arms across the grass to the sidewalk. "The past should stay in the past."

CHAPTER 8

When Nikki woke up the next morning, for a split second she was back in the banquet room, surrounded by people she didn't know, with the sound of the gavel banging through her mind, her heart racing. She blinked, and she was back on the couch. After a few more deep breaths, her heart beat slowed and she sat up. She wiped at her eyes and tried to push the memories away. No, she hadn't remembered anything new, but the memory had made waking up difficult.

Nikki picked up her phone, hoping there might be a text from Quinn on it. Instead there were only news stories about what had occurred the day before.

Nikki closed her eyes and set her phone down. She needed some peace and she also needed some toast. Reluctantly, she climbed off the couch and began her morning routine. She hoped that when she walked the dogs, she would be able to calm down. Instead she continued to check her phone repeatedly, hoping for news. She returned the dogs to their homes and promised to be more enthusiastic the next time. Their wagging tails and eager licks had managed to brighten her mood some, and she hoped that her walk with Sonia and Princess would brighten it even more. But she still had some time before she was due to be there, and she needed to drop her car off at the shop.

Nikki decided to stop by the animal shelter on her way to the shop and see how Petra was holding up after the incident the day before. As she drove in the direction of the animal shelter she thought about the events of the previous day. She recalled the blue coupe in the parking lot, and the man, Miller, on the phone who seemed quite upset. She had no idea if either of them was related to the murder, but her interactions with them stuck out in her mind. Out of all the people she encountered the day before, she felt the most uncomfortable recalling the stranger in the blue coupe, and the man on the phone. Of course, that didn't mean much of anything.

Nikki turned into the parking lot of the animal shelter and noticed that there were quite a few more cars there than usual. She made her way through the main entrance of the shelter, where a gathering of people clustered near the front desk.

"Don't worry, everyone, we have plenty of animals for you to look at." Amanda, a volunteer, smiled at them, then waved to Nikki. "Petra is in the grooming room."

"Thanks." Nikki waved back to her as an excited flutter carried through her heart. It had been a long time since she saw so many people so eager to adopt. She guessed that it had to do with the fundraiser the day before.

Nikki continued down a hallway to an open room that contained a few large sinks. She spotted Petra hunched over one, with Bassie perched inside.

"Bath time, huh?" Nikki grinned as she stepped inside.

"Not sure if it's my bath time, or Bassie's." Petra laughed as the dog splashed her tail through the water.

"How are you doing, Petra?" Nikki paused

beside the sink. "I know yesterday had to be pretty upsetting for you."

"It was." Petra nodded, then glanced up at her. "I didn't expect anything like that to happen. It was a huge shock."

"Yes, it was." Nikki watched as Bassie sloshed around in the water. "But I noticed that there are quite a few potential adopters out there."

"Oh yes, and even more people have called in to ask about animals they've seen on our website. It's fantastic." Petra poured some water over Bassie. "I've got a few people interested in Bassie, actually."

"Aw, I'm so happy for her, but I'm going to miss her, too." Nikki gave the dog's wet back a light pat.

"Me too." Petra sighed.

"I'm glad to hear that the fundraiser helped, though." Nikki leaned against the side of the sink.

"It helped so much. Now we have more than enough to keep the shelter running. I think we actually got more donations than were offered, after the fact." Petra shook her head. "I guess tragedy encourages people to open their wallets."

Petra sighed as she sunk her hands into soapy water and grabbed one of Bassie's paws.

"I have given her too many baths, her skin is

going to dry out, but every time I think I got it all, her feet are all gummed up with dirt again."

"Has she been getting into something outside?" Nikki watched as Petra raised Bassie's paw out of the water and scrubbed at the bottom of it.

"No, she got into something at the fundraiser. I'm pretty sure it's sap." Petra frowned as she released the first paw, then picked up the next. "That stuff is really hard to get out."

"I'm sure it is." Nikki narrowed her eyes. "How would she get that on her paws? There aren't any pine trees around here, and certainly not at the country club."

"I have no idea. I thought maybe it was syrup or honey at first, but it certainly smelled like pine sap." Petra held up Bassie's paw and sniffed. "You can't really smell it at all anymore, but it definitely smelled like sap."

"How strange. And you're sure she got into it at the fundraiser?" Nikki asked.

"I'm sure." Petra nodded. "When I got the dogs home, I found smears of it all over my back seat. Bassie hates to be in a crate in the car, so on the way back I let her sit back there with Spots. It was a pain to get it out of my seat, too. I checked Spots' paws, but he didn't have any on him." She shrugged. "It doesn't make any sense, I know."

"Poor Bassie." Nikki stroked the dog's damp fur. "Don't worry, sweetie, you'll be sticky-free soon enough."

"I hope so." Petra sighed, then wiped her hand across her forehead. She looked over at Nikki as suds dripped from the tight curls that framed her hairline. "I can't thank you enough, Nikki. I know that things turned out terribly, but if it weren't for you doing this, we probably wouldn't be open at the end of the month. With the donations we received, we will be able to operate for years to come."

"That is such a relief." Nikki smiled. "And hearing that Bassie will have a new home, makes me even happier. I'm so glad I stopped by to talk with you. How is Spots doing?"

"Spots has been acting a little strangely, actually." Petra squeezed some of the excess water out of the fur on Bassie's back. "He's been pacing his kennel, and barking. He just won't settle down."

"Maybe I should take him out for a quick jog?" Nikki glanced at her watch. "I have plenty of time."

"Sure, that would be great. It's going to take me some time to get Bassie dried off. Go ahead and take him out. Grant is back there." Petra laughed as

Bassie splashed her with her tail again. "I know that was on purpose."

Nikki grinned as she headed out of the grooming room and continued in the direction of the kennels. She was greeted by one of Grant's favorite songs playing full blast. He always listened to music while cleaning the kennels.

"Hey Grant?" Nikki shouted as loud as she could. "Grant? I'm taking Spots out!"

Nikki didn't hear a response and assumed that he was busy on the other end of the kennels. She walked up to Spots and smiled as he trotted up to the gate. "Hey there, buddy. I hear you're a little restless. Why don't we go for a walk?" She opened the gate and clipped his leash onto his collar. She guided him through the rear door and out into the exercise area. As she did, she almost walked right into Grant.

"Get out of here." Grant shouted at a man, who appeared to be twice his size and about ten years older than the slim twenty-five year old. "I told you not to come here."

"Excuse me." Nikki eased Spots out of the way, who began to bark and lunge at the two men.

"Nikki, sorry, I didn't know you were here."

Grant frowned as he glanced at her, then looked back at the man in front of him. "Go now, Lucas."

"I'm going." The other man held up his hands and smiled. "But you're not going to get rid of me, you know that. We have some things to straighten out." He looked past Grant, at Nikki. "Nice dog you got there. A little feisty, huh?" He smirked at the dog. "Chill out, pup, I'm not someone you should worry about." He gave Grant a sharp slap on his shoulder, then turned and walked away.

"What was that about?" Nikki held Spots' leash tight in her hand.

"Nothing." Grant waved his hand. "It was no big deal."

"Grant, are you sure?" Nikki met his eyes. "If that guy is hassling you, I can get Quinn to help you out."

"Listen to you, are you an honorary cop now?" Grant raised an eyebrow. "No, really, it's nothing. I'm glad that you're getting Spots out. He's been a bundle of nerves all morning."

"Seems that way." Nikki held back her opinion about why he might have been so nervous. Lucas made her nervous, too, and the way that Grant had spoken to him, made her curious.

"I'd better get back to cleaning. We have a lot of

visitors today." Grant nodded to her, then stepped back inside the shelter.

Nikki watched him go, before Spots burst into a run. She laughed as she ran to keep up with him.

"Oh yes, you definitely have some energy to burn off, boy."

CHAPTER 9

Sonia glanced out through the window at the driveway. "There she is, Princess."

She clipped Princess' leash on her, then stepped out through the door to greet Nikki.

"We were wondering when you might arrive. Any news?" Sonia met Nikki's eyes.

"No, nothing yet. I got caught up with Spots at the animal shelter and I had to drop my car off. I do have good news about the animal shelter." Nikki took Princess' leash and began guiding her down the driveway. "The fundraiser has saved the animal shelter, and also drummed up a lot of interest in adoptions."

"That's fantastic. I'm glad to hear it." Sonia smiled to herself. "Well, Daniel, it looks like you managed to help save the day. That's something at least."

"It is." Nikki wrapped her arm around Sonia's shoulders and gave them a quick squeeze. "Now, we need to find out what happened to Daniel. I did discover something last night. Apparently, he had been using a dating app on his phone."

"He was on a dating app?" Sonia rolled her eyes. "Of course, he was. I don't know why that surprises me."

"He had lots of responses." Nikki ushered Princess along the sidewalk. "But there was one woman in particular that seemed to be determined to get in touch with him."

"Geoff Wollers, Daniel's lawyer, mentioned that he'd been breaking more hearts lately. He suspects that it might have been one of those women that killed him." Sonia frowned. "I guess it's possible."

"Did Geoff say who he was seeing?" Nikki glanced over at her, then narrowed her eyes. "Wait a minute, when did you talk to Geoff?"

"Yesterday evening, when I took Princess for a walk." Sonia smiled. "I tried to relax but I couldn't. I needed to get out, to get some fresh air."

"I would have walked with you." Nikki frowned.

"I know, but I didn't want you to have to come

all the way back to me. I also thought Geoff might tell me more if I was alone." Sonia shrugged. "You're not the only one that wants this murder solved."

"I know, but I worry about you—"

"Not that again." Sonia shook her head. "I've told you enough times, Nikki, I'm fully capable of taking care of myself."

"And I've told you, you don't have to, because I'm your friend, and I'm willing to be by your side whenever you might need me or want me to be." Nikki crossed her arms and squinted stubbornly.

"All right, all right. I hear you." Sonia couldn't help but smile some. Although Nikki's tendency to be overprotective of her sometimes made her feel a bit useless, she couldn't deny that she appreciated the friendship they shared. Before she and Nikki had become close, she had plenty of acquaintances, but no one she would consider a close friend. Nikki had changed all of that. "Well, in that case, you might want to come with me to meet Daniel's assistant, Rick. I made an appointment with him today."

"You did?" Nikki nodded. "I'd love to join you. Do you think he'll know something?"

"He was Daniel's personal assistant, but Daniel

mentioned to me that he had only recently hired him, so I don't know if he would have confided in him. Still, he could know something." Sonia picked up a stick and tossed it for Princess to chase. "How did things go with Quinn?"

"I just left him a message. I haven't spoken to him today." Nikki frowned. "I haven't told him about the woman on the dating app. I just feel like he has so much on his plate already, and this could be nothing."

"Or it could be something. Maybe Rick will know something about it." Sonia glanced at her watch. "If we're going to make that meeting, we'd better get going. Are you free to join me?"

"Yes, I already walked the other dogs. I don't have anything on my schedule until their afternoon walk." Nikki guided Princess to turn around and walk back towards the house. "I just hope Quinn's silence means that they're on to something. Maybe they'll have it figured out before the meeting is even over."

"Maybe. We can hope." Sonia smiled. However, she didn't feel the hope she spoke about. Daniel had lived a secretive life. He knew how to hide the truth if he wanted to. It seemed more likely to her, that whoever had taken aim and pulled the trigger, was someone that Daniel would keep under the radar. It might be hard to uncover the truth.

"Yes, we should think positively." Nikki smiled.

"You stay here this time, darling." Sonia took Princess from Nikki's arms and gave her a light kiss on the top of her head. "We won't be long." She tossed a few treats into Princess' bowl, then hurried towards the door. Princess was so busy concentrating on the treats that she barely looked up as Sonia left. "Oh. I do hate leaving her." Sonia frowned.

"She'll be okay." Nikki smiled. "Once I showed up here when she didn't expect me to and she didn't notice me at first. I found her lounging on the couch chewing on the remote."

"What?" Sonia laughed. "Not my Princess!"

"Oh yes." Nikki grinned. "I think she likes her alone time now and then, so she can get into things."

"That makes me wonder where I left the remote." Sonia narrowed her eyes. "She'd better not chew it up."

"Don't worry, I got her a toy that looks like one and hid it under the ottoman." Nikki grinned.

"That's why she's been barking at the ottoman." Sonia laughed as she slid into the driver's seat of her car. "I thought she might be losing her mind."

"Sorry, I meant to tell you." Nikki settled in the passenger seat. "I guess it worked."

"It sure did." Sonia started the car. "His office isn't far from here. I just hope that he's going to be willing to talk to us. I set the appointment claiming that I had a legal matter to discuss with him. I didn't want to be brushed aside."

"Once we're in, we'll get him to talk." Nikki looked out through the windshield at the oncoming traffic. "But first we have to get there. What's with all the traffic?"

"Media, I bet. Daniel was a very wealthy man. The sharks are likely to circle." Sonia managed to find an opening and pulled out onto the road. "Tell me more about this woman on the dating app."

"Her name is Ava Dunn. She said she'd been trying to reach Daniel, and that he'd been avoiding her." Nikki frowned as she pulled out her phone. "I'm opening the app now, maybe I can find out more about her."

"It sounds like Daniel. He did like to avoid his problems, and his emotions." Sonia turned down the street that led to Rick's office.

"It sounds to me like you knew Daniel quite well." Nikki glanced up at her.

"I knew him well enough. When you are in the

same social circle for so long you hear things about each other." Sonia focused on finding the right office building. "Here it is." She turned into the plaza and parked in front of the office that belonged to Rick. "We're a few minutes early, but I don't see any other cars nearby." She frowned as she looked around the parking lot. "Hopefully, he's actually here."

Nikki held open the door for Sonia as she stepped inside. She looked around the small reception area. A few chairs, some old carpeting, and an empty desk. She frowned.

"It looks like he might not be."

"Well, the door was open." Sonia stepped farther in. "Hello? Rick? Are you here?"

The interior door swung open and a man Nikki recognized as Miller stepped through the door. She flashed back to the day before when she saw him with his phone pressed against his ear outside the country club.

"Mrs. Whitter, please come right in." Rick gestured through the door to his office which had a sign 'Rick Miller'.

"Is your receptionist off today?" Sonia led the way into the office.

"Actually, I'm between receptionists right now." Rick sat down at his desk and waved his hand at the

CINDY BELL

two chairs in front of it. "Please, sit. I'd like to hear about this matter with Mr. Barclay."

"There is no matter." Sonia sat down in one of the chairs and looked straight across the desk at him. "I'd like to know what you know about what Daniel was up to during his final days."

"Oh, I see." Rick adjusted his chair, then looked over at Nikki. "And I suppose you'd like to know the same?"

"Yes." Nikki gazed back at him.

"Well, that's a relief. I honestly thought, when I saw the two of you, that I would be faced with a long-lost kid problem. I guess that would be more up Geoff's alley." Rick chuckled.

"She's young enough to be my granddaughter." Sonia shook her head.

"Well, you never know these days." Rick shrugged. "Daniel was a very busy man. He had many appointments on his schedule. It's not really my place to reveal his activities to strangers." He narrowed his eyes as he looked at Sonia. "But you weren't exactly a stranger, were you? I took your call about the auction. He gave me a list of some of his most valuable possessions and told me to make sure they were available for the auction. In two days?" He offered a strained smile. "That was no easy task."

"I'm sure it wasn't." Nikki sat forward in her chair. "But we're more interested in whether he received any other phone calls, or letters, of a threatening nature?"

"Not really, no. Now and then of course there were some disgruntled calls when business deals went wrong, some threatened to sue, some threatened to hunt him down and knock him out." Rick waved his hand. "But nothing serious."

"Have you given the information about all of those threats to the police?" Nikki watched as he nervously moved his phone back and forth on the top of the desk.

"Everything I thought was important, of course." Rick sighed. "No one saw this coming. Daniel had his troubles of course, but nothing that would warrant murder. I mean, no." He shook his head. "Just no."

"What about a love interest?" Sonia tapped her foot lightly against the floor. "Someone new that he was seeing?"

"Not that I know of, but he wasn't always open with me about that part of his life." Rick tilted his head back and forth. "He did order some flowers a couple of weeks ago, but it's hard to say if it was personal, or business."

"Were they for Ava Dunn?" Nikki scooted forward in her chair.

"Uh, let's see." Rick picked up his phone and began to skim through it. "They were for a Martha Rhiner." He looked up at them. "Ordered a couple of weeks ago and delivered to an address north of here." He looked back down at his phone. "No note or anything specific, just his name and telephone number."

"Interesting. Do you know who she is?" Sonia asked.

"No idea." Rick shook his head.

"Could we have that address?" Sonia stood up from her chair.

"What do you need it for?" Rick studied her, his eyes narrowed.

"We're just trying to get an idea of who was important in Daniel's life." Nikki stood up as well. "I would think that someone he sent flowers to, might be important."

"All right, I suppose it couldn't do any harm." Rick jotted down the address on a slip of paper and offered it to Sonia. "Now, unless there is a real legal matter to attend to, I really do have a lot to handle today."

"I'm sure you do." Sonia took the slip of paper. "I'm very sorry for your loss."

"Thank you." Rick cleared his throat. "It hasn't been easy."

"I'm sure." Nikki nodded and offered him a sad smile. "Thank you for your time." She led the way out of the office, and back to the car. On the way to the car Nikki quietly explained to Sonia how she had seen Rick outside the country club the previous day and the conversation she had overheard.

"That's interesting. It might be worth exploring more, but now we have another lead to follow." Sonia nodded. "Shall we go see who this Martha person is?" She opened the driver's side door.

"Let's do it." Nikki smiled as she buckled into the passenger seat. She checked her phone again. Nothing from Quinn. She decided to send him the information she'd discovered, just in case he didn't have it. With his resources, he could probably easily find out if Ava Dunn or Martha Rhiner had a solid connection to Daniel. As she typed out the message, she hoped that she wouldn't be interrupting something important.

"The address isn't far. Actually, it's in my

neighborhood." Sonia started the car, then drove out of the parking lot. "I wonder what his connection to Martha was?"

"Maybe she'll be willing to tell us." Nikki hit send on the text, then sat back against the seat. Now, it would be hard to be patient and wait for a response from him. "It sounds to me like Daniel had a lot going on that no one else knew about."

"Yes, it does." Sonia navigated her way through Dahlia, then pulled up to a house about ten minutes away from hers. "It looks like this is the place." She peered at the entrance to the long driveway. "No security gate, that's a good thing."

"No security gate, and apparently no gardener." Nikki studied the overgrown bushes and long grass that they drove past. "That's pretty unusual for this part of Dahlia. I'm surprised it's been allowed."

"The property is set so far back from the road, I bet no one even notices it." Sonia huffed. "But this place needs a good cleaning up. I wonder why she let it get this bad?"

"Maybe she's going through a hard time." Nikki frowned as Sonia parked in front of the house. "What's that on the front porch?" She stepped out of the car and walked towards it. "Oh wow, Sonia, I think these are the flowers that were delivered." She picked up a wilted plant in a basket. "I guess she never got them?"

Nikki looked at the note attached. It had Daniel's details on it.

"I guess not." Sonia walked past her and knocked on the front door. "Hello? Is anyone home?" She peeked through the window beside the door. "It doesn't look like anyone has lived here in a while."

"We should go." Nikki frowned. "I'll let Quinn know. I'm sure he'll come and check the place out."

"Good idea." Sonia walked back to the car. "Whoever Martha is, she isn't going to want those flowers now."

Nikki glanced back at the house as Sonia drove off. Obviously, Daniel had believed that Martha still lived there, which meant that he might not have been in recent contact with her. So, why did he suddenly want to send her flowers? Did it have something to do with why he had been acting so secretive lately?

CHAPTER 10

On the way back to Sonia's house, Nikki's cell phone buzzed. She glanced down at her phone and smiled at the sight of a text from Quinn.

"Quinn wants me to meet him at Gina's for a coffee." Nikki sent a quick text in response. "Hopefully he has some news." She tucked her phone into her purse. "Do you want to join us?"

"I wouldn't dream of it." Sonia winked. "I'll drop you off." She activated her turn signal.

"No, don't do that. You're already almost home, and I'm sure that Princess can't wait to see you. I can walk. It's a beautiful afternoon."

"Are you sure? I don't mind."

"I know you don't, but it's okay. It's not a far walk." Nikki smiled.

"Okay, but you'd better update me as soon as you can." Sonia turned into her driveway, then parked.

"I will, as soon as I know anything." Nikki waved to her, then headed down the driveway. She quickened her pace as she reached the street. She couldn't wait to see Quinn, and not just because she hoped he had news, but because she always enjoyed being with him. However, she wanted to walk to help keep her nerves at bay. Being around Quinn still stirred a sense of awkwardness and giddiness within her that always left her feeling a little embarrassed. Exercise helped her to reduce the anxiety that plagued her when she thought about being alone with him. She enjoyed the time with him, but she just couldn't quite relax. She hoped she would get used to being in his presence so that she would be able to relax in it soon.

Nikki continued towards Gina's, a café owned by her good friend Gina. Nikki would usually be excited to see her and get the latest gossip, but she knew her friend wouldn't be there. She was having a couple of days off. It was the first time since Nikki had known her that she had taken time off. Her parents were visiting from out of town, so after a lot of persuading she agreed to leave her business in her employees' hands for a few days. Nikki was sure that Gina still checked in with them at every opportunity.

When Nikki had almost reached the café, her phone buzzed again. She pulled it out of her purse and read the message from Quinn.

Are you on your way?

Nikki sent a quick text back.

I'm here.

As Nikki looked up at the front door of Gina's, it swung open. Quinn stepped out with two coffee cups and strode over to her.

"I'm glad you're here." Quinn gestured to the sidewalk. "Let's take a quick walk." He handed her a coffee.

"Thank you." Nikki smiled. "Don't you want to go inside?" She looked past him at the door.

"I don't want to discuss this inside. I have news and questions. And I feel like a walk." Quinn caught her hand and led her down the sidewalk. "That name you gave me, Ava Dunn? How did you come across that?"

"Oh, I found it when I was doing some research on Daniel." Nikki shrugged.

"Research? Why doesn't that surprise me!" Quinn shook his head. "Well, it was a good lead. I looked into it, and it turns out that Ava Dunn, isn't who she says she is." His voice tightened.

Nikki glanced over at him. Was he nervous, too? Or upset? She couldn't tell.

"What do you mean? She was using a fake name?" Nikki looked at her phone as it rang. "Sorry Quinn, it's a client." She grimaced. "I have to take this."

Quinn smiled and nodded as she answered the call.

"Vera." Nikki held the phone to her ear.

"Nikki." Vera's panicked voice replied. "I'm so glad I managed to reach you."

"Why?" Nikki's heartbeat raced from the urgency in her voice. "Is Sassy okay?"

"Yes, she's okay." Vera spoke quickly. "But I tripped down my stairs and I hurt my ankle."

"Oh no. Are you okay?" Nikki cringed.

"I am, but Sassy is at the groomers in Magnolia and I can't pick her up. I'm at the hospital, getting an X-ray." Vera's voice wavered. "Sassy hates the groomers and I have no one else I can ask. She needs to be picked up before they close. They are only open until two today."

"Oh Vera." Nikki sighed. "My car is in the shop."

"Oh no." The woman burst into tears.

Nikki knew that Vera could be very high strung, especially when it came to Sassy.

"It's going to be okay." Nikki grimaced. "Let me see what I can do, and I'll call you back."

"Thank you." Vera's voice lightened slightly. Nikki ended the call.

"What's wrong?" Quinn squeezed Nikki's hand. Nikki explained the situation.

"I'll have to see if I can borrow Sonia's car." Nikki frowned.

"I'll give you a lift." Quinn offered.

"You don't have to do that." Nikki smiled slightly. "You have to work."

"I want to, that way I can update you on the way. I could use a break." Quinn turned towards the car park. "I am waiting for some information to come through anyway."

"Thank you." Nikki followed Quinn towards his car as she informed a very relieved Vera that she was going to pick up Sassy. After they had settled in, she turned towards him.

"So, Ava Dunn is a fake name?"

"Not just a fake name. A fake gender and

persona. Ava Dunn, is a man, named Malcolm Hera. We're still looking into his motive, but apparently he's been stalking Daniel on more than one platform." Quinn narrowed his eyes as he studied her. "We came across Ava's profile on a dating app."

"Wow. I never even considered that possibility." Stunned, Nikki's mind swam with the knowledge that Ava was a man. "Do you think Daniel knew she was a man?"

"I have no idea." Quinn started the car.

"But if Ava is actually Malcolm, then you need to find him. Do you know where he is?" Nikki turned towards him.

"No, we are tracking him down." Quinn frowned as he pulled into traffic. "We tracked Ava Dunn's online activity. That's how we were able to trace it back to Malcolm. But I'm still waiting for his address to come through."

"Okay? That's great that you got a lead from it. That's why I gave you the names, I knew with your resources you'd be able to find out much more than I could. Oh, by the way, we happened to drive past Martha's house. It looked like it hadn't been lived in for a long time. Did you find anything out about her?" Nikki frowned.

"Happened to drive past?" Quinn raised his eyebrows as he turned on his turn signal and pulled to a stop in the parking lot of the groomers. "No, we haven't found any information, yet." He turned towards her. "Nikki, I need to ask you something?"

"Of course." Nikki smiled.

"I thought you and I were going to see where this relationship was going. I guess, I never really asked you if you were seeing other people." Quinn sighed, then met her eyes and took her hand.

"What?" Nikki's heart jumped into her throat. "What are you talking about? Of course, I'm not seeing other people."

"So, you can imagine why I was surprised when Ava Dunn wasn't the only person that had been looking at Daniel's profile on the app. Another member was, you." Quinn narrowed his eyes.

"Sure, I was looking at it, how else do you think I found Ava?" Nikki's eyes widened as she looked at him. "Oh! Oh no!" She laughed and groaned at the same time. "Quinn, did you think it was a real profile? I mean, that I was on a dating app?"

"Well I—" He frowned. "I wasn't sure what to think."

"Quinn." Nikki took his hand and held it firmly. "I only made the profile to find out information

111

about Daniel. It wouldn't let me surf the site without creating a profile. That's how I found out about Ava. She left a comment in the ratings section."

"Wow." Quinn winced. "I guess I look pretty foolish right now."

"Not at all." Nikki smiled as she swept her fingertips along the curve of his cheek. "You're adorable when you're jealous."

"I wasn't exactly jealous." Quinn caught her hand.

"No?" Nikki smiled as he looked into her eyes.

"Yes, madly." Quinn kissed the back of her hand then sighed. "I'm sorry. I've been asking you to trust me, and I just jumped to a ridiculous conclusion, didn't I?"

"It's all right." Nikki laughed.

"You better get Sassy before she gets too upset." Quinn blushed. Nikki leaned over and kissed his cheek.

"I won't be long."

CHAPTER 11

*A*fter a few minutes, Nikki returned to the car with a very happy Sassy in tow. Sassy was a medium-sized dog with big, floppy ears and curly, white fur. Her fur looked especially shiny because she had just been freshly groomed. Nikki popped open the back door and Sassy hopped up on the back seat. Before Nikki could stop her, Sassy leaned through the gap between the front seats and gave Quinn a lick on his cheek. Nikki cringed when she realized Quinn was on the phone.

"Sorry about that." She grimaced as she got in the car after he ended the call.

"It's okay. She's a sweet girl." Quinn leaned back and patted Sassy's head. "I am going to have to take you back quickly." He frowned.

"Okay. Why?"

"I just found out where Malcolm lives." Quinn started the car.

"You did?"

"He lives in a remote cabin just about an hour and a half from here. About two hours from Dahlia." Quinn backed the car up. "He runs a campground there."

"Oh?" Nikki stared at him. "Well, why don't we come with you?"

"You can't." Quinn shook his head.

"Why not?" Nikki smiled. "It will save you time."

"Are you sure?" Quinn asked. "What about Sassy? It's a long drive."

"Absolutely. She's great in the car." Nikki nodded. "I just have to tell Vera."

"But you can't come in to see Malcolm, of course." Quinn pulled the car to a stop and looked at her.

"Of course." Nikki smiled as she sent Vera a text. "It will be fun. A road trip."

"Okay." Quinn smiled as he pulled the car onto the road.

"Great." Nikki nodded then reached for the radio.

"No wait, I like that song." Quinn waved her hand away from the buttons on the radio as he kept his eyes on the road.

"Really? This song?" Nikki tried not to laugh as the pop song blasted through his speakers.

"Nothing wrong with a little pick-me-up music." Quinn glanced over at Nikki and smiled. "You don't like it?"

"I like that it makes you smile." Nikki grinned, then settled back in her seat. "You know, I keep thinking about that empty house that belonged to Martha, and the flowers that Daniel had delivered to her. Something just doesn't feel right about it?"

"I think you're right. My guys are on it, but they haven't been able to locate Martha yet." Quinn turned off the highway onto a smaller road.

"Do you think she is dead?" Nikki frowned. "Maybe he didn't know."

"There weren't any death records for her, but it's still possible. Sometimes things happen, and deaths aren't recorded." Quinn turned on the windshield wipers as a spate of rain struck the windshield.

"That's so sad, the thought that she could have died, and no one reported it." Nikki sighed. "Maybe we have another mystery to unravel."

"We?" Quinn shot a look over at her.

"Maybe I should join the police academy." Nikki grinned.

"No." Quinn turned off onto another even smaller road, and the buildings they had been driving past were replaced by open fields.

"No?" Nikki laughed. "Just no?"

"I mean, you can do whatever you want, of course." Quinn licked his lips, then shook his head. "But no."

"That's not a full sentence you know, it's just a word." Nikki raised an eyebrow.

"I just wouldn't want you to be in danger." As the speed limit lowered, Quinn slowed the car and began to scan the road signs they passed.

"That's sweet." Nikki smiled as she looked at him.

"Now, where is that road?" Quinn cleared his throat as he leaned forward and squinted through the windshield. "There's his road." He turned the wheel hard to make the turn in time.

Nikki slid in her seat and braced herself against the dashboard. When they were safely on the new road, Nikki looked over at him.

"Here it is." Quinn turned down a narrow dirt road that led up to several rows of cabins. He parked in a small parking lot off to the side of one of the larger cabins. "You stay in the car."

"I need to take Sassy out for a bit."

"Okay, but you can't come into the cabin, you need to stay quiet and out of sight."

"Of course."

"I mean it, Nikki." Quinn glanced back at her as he stepped out of the car.

"Of course, quiet." Nikki made a zipping gesture across her lips. "And out of sight."

Quinn nodded, then strode towards the door of the cabin. As he reached it, he brushed his suit jacket back, and adjusted his gun in its holster, then he let the jacket fall forward again. He opened the door of the cabin and stepped inside.

Nikki watched him, then turned her attention to Sassy. She grabbed Sassy's leash and the dog jumped down off the back seat. She pulled a bottle of water and a collapsible bowl out of her backpack and poured some water in the bowl for her to drink.

After Sassy had a few sips, the eager dog started sniffing and led Nikki around the side of the cabin. Nikki let Sassy guide her. As Sassy stopped to sniff a tree, Nikki looked in a window of the cabin that was slightly open. She noticed Quinn walk up to the desk just as a man stepped into the room. She presumed that the man must be Malcolm. She stood to the side of the window so she was out of view but could still see through the window.

The cabin was set up as a main office for the campground. There were several displays around the room featuring local animal life and flora. A large desk took up one side of the cabin, and the man stepped behind it.

"Welcome." He smiled at Quinn. "Is there anything I can help you with? Were you interested in renting a cabin?"

Nikki held her breath. She had a full view of everything, but if Quinn caught her, he would be furious. The man's mop of dark curls, and warm smile, didn't exactly make him look like a threat.

"Actually, I have a few questions for you." Quinn revealed his badge and introduced himself, then looked straight at the man. "Malcolm Hera?"

"Yes." Malcolm's eyes widened.

"Do you know a man named Daniel Barclay?"

"Oh, uh." Malcolm took a step back. "Why?"

"Just answer the question please." Quinn rested his hands on the desk that separated the two of them.

"Yes, I know him." Malcolm frowned. "What is all of this about?"

"Could you tell me why you were stalking Daniel under the name, Ava Dunn?"

"I'm not stalking him. Not exactly." Malcolm shifted from one foot to the other as he stared at Quinn.

"But you admit to using a false name in an attempt to contact him?" Quinn locked his eyes to Malcolm's. "Why did you do that, Malcolm?"

"Why are you asking me these questions?" Malcolm shook his head. "Is Daniel in some kind of trouble or something?"

"I'd like you to answer my question, Malcolm. What is your connection to Daniel Barclay?" Quinn's voice hardened.

Nikki held tightly to Sassy's leash as the dog eagerly sniffed. Nikki sensed the tension growing between the two men. Would Malcolm bolt? Would he try to fight Quinn? Her heart pounded.

"The truth is, Daniel is my father." Malcolm frowned. "I made up Ava Dunn as a way to try to reach out to him, without him knowing who I was. That's not against the law is it?"

CHAPTER 12

*M*alcolm's confession knocked the wind from Nikki's body. She stared at him through the window, her eyes wide, and her teeth clenched. If Daniel was his father, and he had no idea why Quinn was there, that meant he had no idea that his father had been killed. In his remote cabin, she guessed that he didn't keep up with the latest news.

"You're sure he's your father?" Quinn's voice remained steady.

"Yes, we had a paternity test done." Malcolm sighed. "Look, when I was a kid, I had no idea who my father was. My mother always told me that he was a nobody, and that I needed to forget about him. So, I did. But as I got older, I got more and more curious. Finally, she told me his name. When she did, I started looking into him." He rolled his eyes. "Imagine my surprise when I discovered how wealthy he was. Then of course, you'll probably think I wanted some of his money. But I didn't. I'm happy here. I have everything I need. I have everything I want." He shook his head. "I can't expect you to understand. I just wanted to know who I looked like, why I have a tendency to avoid relationships. I just wanted to see if he was anything like me."

"And did you?" Quinn pulled out his notepad and began to jot down a few notes. "Were you able to make contact with him?"

"Yes, I was. Of course, he wanted the DNA test first, so we did that. Then he got more friendly." Malcolm shrugged and glanced down at the desk. "I thought he was happy to hear from me. He seemed to want to meet up. Then all of a sudden, he stopped taking my calls. I haven't been able to reach him. I figured he'd just changed his mind." He squinted at Quinn. "Are you ever going to tell me what this is all about? I mean, am I in some kind of trouble?"

"That depends. Where were you yesterday between ten and twelve?" Quinn's shoulders straightened.

Nikki studied Malcolm's reaction to the question.

"Where was I?" Malcolm's eyes widened. "I was here. I'm always here."

"Any witnesses to prove that?" Quinn's pen hovered over his notepad.

"Squirrels. Maybe a few deer." Malcolm chuckled, then his laughter faded. "You're serious, aren't you?"

"Yes, I am." Quinn set the notepad down. "Did you see or speak to anyone during those times?"

"Uh, ten to twelve. Well, I usually do a walk of the campsites around ten. But we didn't have too many campers yesterday. I don't know, maybe?" Malcolm ran his hand back through his hair.

"Maybe? You can't tell me if you spoke to anyone yesterday?" Quinn narrowed his eyes.

"I think I did. I mean, I know I did, I'm just not sure what time it was. Around here, we don't exactly keep track of time." Malcolm stepped around the side of the desk. "Now you need to tell me what this is about. Why does it matter where I was?"

"I'm a homicide detective, investigating the murder of Daniel Barclay." Quinn took a step closer to him. "He was killed yesterday in Dahlia."

"What?" Malcolm stumbled back.

Nikki held her hand over her mouth to hide a gasp. She wanted to help him.

"I'm sorry for your loss." Quinn looked at him.

"This can't be true." Malcolm looked at Quinn. "It can't be!"

"I'm afraid it is." Quinn shifted closer. "I'll need a detailed statement about your whereabouts and activities yesterday. Would you like to give that to me here, or would you like for me to arrange for you to come to Dahlia?"

"What?" Malcolm stared at him.

"I need to know where you would like to give me a statement?" Quinn's voice sharpened.

"What?" Malcolm repeated.

"I know it's a shock." Quinn's voice softened slightly. "Here, Malcolm, why don't you sit down." He pulled a stool from one of the displays over and guided Malcolm down onto it. "Would you like a drink of water?"

"No." Malcolm's shoulders jerked as he shivered. "He's dead? You're sure?" He met Quinn's eyes.

"Yes. I'm sure. If it's easier, I can record your statement." Quinn pulled out his phone.

"Wait." Malcolm took a shaky breath. "If you

want to know where I was, that means, you suspect me? You think I killed my own father?"

"I'm just gathering information right now, Malcolm." Quinn eyed him with some authority. "The best way for me to find your father's killer is to know the whereabouts of the people in his life."

"You mean, the potential suspects." Malcolm shook his head and took a step back. "I'm not saying another word. Not without a lawyer."

"Malcolm, you can either talk to me here, or I can get a warrant, and you can talk to me two hours from here. Which is it going to be?" Quinn stared straight into his eyes.

"I told you where I was. I have nothing else to say. If that means that you need to arrest me, then arrest me." Malcolm held his hands out in front of him. "But I don't think you can. You have no reason to suspect me. I know you don't, because I know I'm innocent. So, as far as I'm concerned, this conversation is over, and I would like you to leave."

"Thank you for your time, Malcolm. You will be hearing from me again, very soon." Quinn held his gaze a moment longer, then turned towards the door.

Nikki ran to the car with Sassy and quickly put

her in the car, just as Quinn opened the door to the cabin.

Once Nikki and Quinn were settled in the car, Quinn started it and explained to Nikki what he had discovered as he steered the car down the dirt driveway. She was relieved that he was forthcoming with the information, so she didn't have to pretend she didn't know what was going on, or admit that she had been eavesdropping.

"It must have been terrible to have to break the news to Malcolm." Nikki frowned as she looked over at Quinn.

"It's not the easiest thing to have to do." Quinn grimaced. "But it's news that you only get to deliver once, and as a detective it's better to deliver it bluntly so that you get a clear reaction. I can tell a lot by the way someone reacts to bad news."

"What did you find out about Malcolm when you told him?"

"Actually, he seemed genuinely shocked. However, I can't pin everything on that reaction. He had plenty of time to practice it and get it just right. The fact that he went straight from telling me where he was, to wanting to get a lawyer, tells me that he probably has something to hide." Quinn turned onto the main road.

"It's terrible that the two of them reunited, only to be separated again."

"I'm not so sure it's the sweet story you're picturing." Quinn continued down the highway towards Dahlia. "It's not likely that a man like Daniel Barclay would go decades without knowing that he has a child out there. I'm sure he knew about Malcolm."

"If he did, then why didn't he contact him? Why would he act happy to find him then start ignoring him?" Nikki frowned.

"Maybe he wasn't happy to find him. The only person who has said that, is Malcolm. Maybe Daniel actually rejected him when Malcolm reached out to him, and Malcolm decided to kill him." Quinn turned onto the main road that ran through Dahlia. "The point is, even if things seem one way, we can't assume that it's the way things happened."

"Yes, I'm sure you're right about that." Nikki pursed her lips. She wanted Malcolm to be innocent because she liked the story he told. But that might not be the case.

"I'll take you to drop Sassy off, then take you home." Quinn switched into the turning lane as he approached a red light.

"No, it's okay. I'd rather walk. Sassy will

appreciate the walk after the long drive. Just go ahead back to the station, I know that you have a ton of work to do, especially with this news." Nikki gave his arm a pat as he switched lanes again. "Thanks for helping me out with Sassy."

"No problem." Quinn pulled into the parking lot of the police station, then put the car in park. "Nikki, I hope you understand, I may seem harsh, but it's my job to be impartial."

"I do." Nikki leaned over and kissed his cheek. As she opened the car door, she noticed her foot stuck to the carpet a bit. "Ugh, I think I got some sap on my shoe." She frowned as she wiped it against the pavement of the parking lot. "Hopefully, it will come off on the walk home."

"Not likely." Quinn shook his head. "Sap likes to stick around."

"Cute, very cute." Nikki laughed and grabbed Sassy's leash as she jumped out of the car.

She gave Quinn a quick wave before they walked down the sidewalk. It certainly had been an interesting afternoon.

CHAPTER 13

*S*onia hung up the phone and sighed. She'd spent a lot of time calling friends and business contacts to find out what she could about Martha but had turned up nothing. She had hoped that she would have a new lead to share with Nikki. Instead she had what felt like a dead end. She hoped that Nikki might have discovered something better.

As Sonia walked past the piano in the corner of the large living room, she paused beside it. She could recall a time when she had friends over just about every evening. Someone would play the piano. Someone else would pour the wine. Daniel had been there many times. She could remember his laughter carrying over the melodic notes of the piano. She could remember his smile, the way he flashed it at anyone he wanted to charm. Her thoughts shifted to that horrible moment when Daniel fell to his knees. She hadn't even heard the gunshot. How was that possible? The thought made her head swim with criticisms and worries. Was her hearing failing? Was she just so fixated on the vase that she blocked out everything else? She had been right there beside him, and yet she was unable to help him.

A knock on the front door jolted her out of her thoughts.

"Sonia? I'm here to walk Princess." Nikki called out.

Sonia looked towards the door, took a slow breath, then turned and walked towards it. She smiled as she opened the door for her.

"Nikki, I'm so glad you came by. Princess is restless." Sonia led her inside. "Do you mind taking her for a walk alone? I'm a little worn out myself."

"Not a problem at all." Nikki reached for Princess' leash which hung on a hook near the front door.

"Wait, not until you dish." Sonia smiled. "You spent all afternoon with Quinn, I know you know something."

"Unfortunately, I don't know a whole lot. But we did discover something pretty interesting." Nikki filled Sonia in on Malcolm being Daniel's son.

"Are you sure about that?" Sonia shook her head. "It doesn't sound like Daniel."

"You don't think after all of those years of playing the field there could have been a slip up?" Nikki pursed her lips.

"Oh no, I'm sure there could have been. But if there was, Daniel would have taken care of the child. He would have wanted to be part of his life." Sonia sat down on the couch and sighed. "He didn't want to have children, but I do believe that if he'd had one, he would have doted over the child."

"You said yourself that you didn't really know him that well." Nikki sat down beside her. "Don't you think it's possible that you're mistaken about this."

"I guess it's possible. But it just seems wrong." Sonia clutched her hands together. "Daniel loved kids, he would play with them every chance he got. He just didn't want to add to the population. Sometimes I thought he regretted not having one of his own. It just seems off to me."

"Maybe Malcolm's mother never told him?" Nikki nodded slowly. "Malcolm said that his mother didn't tell him who his father was until a short time ago. He did say that Daniel had communicated with him for a while, so it wasn't as if he rejected Malcolm straight away."

"And who is Malcolm's mother?" Sonia looked over at Nikki. "Maybe I know her."

"Actually, I don't know." Nikki shook her head. "Quinn never asked that question. I guess that's something we could try to figure out, though I'm not even sure where to start. I don't think that Malcolm is going to be willing to speak to us about anything at all." She sighed as she recalled the way that he ended his conversation with Quinn. "He told Quinn he wouldn't say another word without a lawyer. He seems to be hiding something."

"That's all right, Malcolm isn't our only option to find out the truth." Sonia pursed her lips. "Leave it to me, Nikki, I can find out who she is."

"I'm sure you can." Nikki nodded. "But are you sure you want to do this?"

"Absolutely." Sonia smiled. "And it means a lot to me that you're helping."

"Of course." Nikki shook her head. "I wouldn't even hesitate. We need to find out what happened that day." Her voice faltered, and she glanced sharply away.

"Nikki?" Sonia looked into Nikki's eyes. "Are you all right?"

"I'm sorry." Nikki pressed her hand against her chest as she took a breath. "It's just that when I think of that moment, I can't help but think of how close you were standing next to Daniel, how if that bullet had strayed even the slightest." She shook her head. "I don't even want to imagine it, but it's all I can think about."

"Oh sweetheart." Sonia hugged her. "I appreciate that you care so much, I do, but it's time to let go of that." She leaned back and looked into Nikki's eyes. "You and I, we're both still here. I'm okay."

"I'm so glad you are." Nikki forced a smile. "I know, I'm letting my emotions get out of control. I need to focus."

"It's okay to be concerned. I think I'll be uneasy until we find out who did this. At least then, I'll be able to have some closure." Sonia squeezed Nikki's hand. "So, let's do just that. Let's go back to basics. What do we know about that day that can lead us to a suspect?"

"Only two things stick out in my mind. A blue coupe that was blocking the cars in the parking lot, and Rick on his way into the country club. He sounded so upset with whoever he was talking to on the phone." Nikki shrugged as she looked at Sonia. "It's not a lot to go on, though."

"It might lead to something."

"Quinn is going to try and confirm that Malcolm was Daniel's son. I think he'll bring him in for questioning and try and get a DNA test organized. If he manages to get a DNA test done, he'll have to wait for the results. All of that is going to take time and might lead nowhere. We might as well try to rule out any other suspects in the meantime."

"What about this blue coupe? Do you know who drove it? Did you get his license plate?" Sonia leaned forward.

"No, unfortunately not. I didn't recognize him either. It was probably nothing, but I just can't shake the memory of it. He parked right in the middle of the parking lot during the auction." Nikki crossed her arms. "I guess it could be a bit of road rage on my part."

"Well, there's no way we can find out more about it right now, so that leaves us with Rick. It can't hurt to talk to him again." Sonia looked up at the clock on the wall. "He should still be in his office."

"I'll take Princess for her walk, then we can

head over." Nikki turned on her heel and headed for the door with Princess at her side.

Sonia watched her go. She felt a ripple of gratitude, paired with a sense of nervous anticipation. Digging into Daniel's life was fascinating in some ways. But knowing how far she'd drifted apart from someone she once considered a friend, was a hard pill to swallow. She hoped that would never be the case between her and Nikki.

CHAPTER 14

On the way back from the park, Nikki became aware of a car on the road. It didn't roll past her, as she expected. Instead it drifted a few feet behind her. She slowed down a little, as Princess explored some grass nearby. Once she got the dog moving again, she realized the car had slowed even more. A quick glance over her shoulder revealed it was a bright blue coupe. Was it the same one? She briefly met the eyes of the driver, and a jolt of fear carried through her. It was the same man behind the wheel, she was sure of it. Was he following her?

"Let's go, Princess." Nikki quickened her pace. When she glanced back over her shoulder again, she watched the car turn into Geoff's driveway. Maybe he was following her, or maybe he was just looking for Geoff's house.

Nikki scooped Princess up and carried her as she turned around and crept closer to Geoff's house. She heard the car door slam, then she heard a flurry of angry words.

"You're not going to get away with this!" The stranger shouted.

"I've already called the police. You have no right to be on my property!" Geoff shot back. "You have less than two minutes to get out of here, or you're going to end up in handcuffs, today. Is that what you want, Sylvester?"

"You know what I want! I want my money!" Sylvester's voice grew even louder.

Nikki clutched Princess tighter against her and watched as the two men faced off not far from Geoff's front door.

"I told you I would handle it." Geoff stepped closer to him. His tone became soothing. "I told you that you would be taken care of, you just need to give it a little time. Everything will get straightened out. With Daniel dead, things are a little chaotic, but it will all calm down."

"It better." Sylvester balled his hands into fists. "I'm tired of being patient."

"Just a little bit longer." Geoff glanced down the road as sirens blared in the distance. "Get out of here now, Sylvester, or you are going to be asked a lot of questions that you don't want to answer."

Nikki gulped as Sylvester turned back towards the car. She felt his gaze skip over her. Had he noticed her? Did he know that she was eavesdropping? She decided not to wait around to find out. She took a shortcut through one of the neighboring properties to get back to Sonia's house quickly.

"Nikki, are you okay?" Sonia met her in the driveway. "You were gone longer than I expected."

"I'm sorry." Nikki filled her in on what she'd just seen, as she let Princess loose in the house. "I think we need to find out what Sylvester's connection to Geoff and Daniel is. He seems angry enough to want to cause some trouble."

"Maybe Rick will know something about him." Sonia led the way to her car. "Hopefully, we'll get something out of him either way."

"It sounds like he might have been an investor or a business partner of some kind." Nikki settled in the passenger seat. As she buckled in, she wondered how many other people they might encounter that had a big problem with Daniel. It seemed to her that he had many enemies, and very few friends. Nikki glanced over at Sonia as she pulled into the parking lot of Rick's office. At least he had one friend that was on his side.

When they stepped into the office, Rick rushed past them to grab some papers from the printer behind an empty desk.

"Yes? What can I help you with?" He tucked the papers into an envelope and set it on the desk.

"Rick, we were hoping you could help us out by telling us what you remember about Sunday. About Daniel in particular, and where you were in the room when he was shot." Nikki wasted no time getting to the point. Maybe if she didn't give him too much time to think about it, she had a better chance of getting the truth.

"What? Why?" Rick glared at her. "Why would I want to remember that?"

"We're just trying to get a better understanding of what happened that day." Nikki took a few steps forward but maintained enough distance not to make him uncomfortable. "Mrs. Whitter and I just tried to recreate the morning, just to try to jog our memories. Then I realized I remembered seeing you going inside. And it occurred to me that you might remember something. Maybe you saw someone out of place?" She met his eyes. "You were there when the shot was fired, weren't you? Do you remember where you were standing?"

"Of course, I was there." Rick crossed his arms. "I was his assistant. It was my job to be everywhere that he was."

"I understand that." Nikki stared into his eyes. "But I'm asking you exactly where were you in the banquet room at the time that Daniel was shot?"

"Oh, I wasn't inside." Rick shrugged. "I had to run back to the truck to grab a piece from the collection that my incompetent laborer overlooked." He rolled his eyes. "He wouldn't know art if it punched him in the face. Anyway, I ducked outside I don't know, for maybe seconds." He closed his eyes briefly, then shook his head. "I stepped back in, and I heard the commotion. I never heard a gunshot."

"You stepped back in after the shot had been fired?" Nikki's eyes narrowed.

"Yes, as far as I know it must have been. Daniel was already on the floor. I thought maybe he'd had a heart attack or a stroke. It wasn't until I saw him that I realized he had been shot." Rick sighed. "Then everyone rushed towards me, heading for the door."

"Wait a minute." Sonia locked her eyes to his. "What about in that moment when you were trying to figure out what happened to Daniel? Did anyone rush past you then?"

"Uh." Rick took a slow breath. "Yes, someone did. I didn't even notice because I was trying to make sense of what was happening. But I felt him bump into my shoulder as he pushed past me."

"Him? Who?" Nikki stepped closer as her heart pounded. Maybe they had just stumbled upon the killer. Why would anyone rush out of the room before they knew what had happened?

"It was uh, Geoff Wollers." Rick nodded. "Yes, I remember now. It was Geoff." Rick looked up at Nikki. "He said something about getting help."

"Oh." Nikki's excitement deflated. Of course, that made sense. Geoff would react to Daniel's collapse with the urge to get help. He probably hadn't heard the shot either. "No one else? What about this man?" She held up her phone with a picture on display of Malcolm that she had managed to get from the website for the campground. "Do you remember seeing him?"

"Let's see." Rick took the phone from her hand and stared at the picture. "He does look a little familiar. But I don't think I saw him in the banquet room, or at all that day. To be honest, I don't think I saw many people. I was in such a frenzy to get everything ready, and my stress level was through the roof. My phone wouldn't stop ringing." He rolled his eyes.

"I noticed that you seemed a little upset over a phone call you received." Nikki chose her words carefully. She didn't want to tip him off to the fact that she suspected him due to that phone call.

"Yes well, some people are impatient." Rick sighed, then handed the phone back to her. "I'm not sure what the point of all of this is. I've already told the police everything I know. I'm sorry that Daniel is gone, but there's not much I can do to help."

"We appreciate whatever information you can give." Sonia smiled some. "How long had you been working with Daniel?"

"Not for too long. A little over four months. He had a high turnover of his assistants. His demands could be a little extreme." Rick grimaced. "I didn't mind them, but he did expect a lot."

"How so?" Sonia narrowed her eyes.

"Mostly, he wanted discretion. He wanted his private life protected. Especially recently. I did the best I could, but it wasn't always the easiest thing to provide. He wanted his privacy, but he had no problem generating a ton of attention by spontaneously participating in a charity auction." Rick frowned. "It was difficult to get everything prepared for that, and field the onslaught of questions as to why he was doing it. He had been refusing to even show his collection lately, let alone donate much of it."

"Why do you think he did it?" Sonia asked.

"He did it for you." Rick locked his eyes to hers. "That was another thing I was supposed to keep to myself. But I guess it doesn't matter now." He shrugged. "You knew that, didn't you?"

"No." Sonia sighed, then clasped her hands together. "Why do you think he wanted so much privacy all of a sudden? I noticed as I was contacting his friends that he hadn't had much interaction with anyone lately. Rick, what was really going on?"

"There was a lot going on with him. A lot of tension. Business deals that went wrong, at least for his partners." Rick frowned. "It was hard to keep up with, and he seemed intent on not telling me everything."

"What about a man named Sylvester?" Nikki met his eyes. "Did you ever hear that name?"

"Sylvester, yes, that was one that he couldn't

hide from me. He planned a big project with Sylvester and a few other investors, but he put a hold on it about a month ago. No explanation, just said he wasn't going to do it anymore." Rick rolled his eyes. "You can't imagine the fallout from that."

"And he never said why?" Sonia shook her head. "There must have been a reason. He was a shrewd businessman. He would never let go of a good deal."

"You're right about that, you seemed to know him well." Rick chuckled. "However, Daniel was incredibly cunning. It was a multimillion dollar deal and he took people for everything they had, including Sylvester and the other investors. He didn't plan to return the money they'd put in, claimed he couldn't get it back. It was in the deal and it was a risk they took, and they knew that when they signed up. When I tried to reason with him, he threatened to fire me." He pursed his lips, then sighed. "No, he wasn't a golden boy, that's for sure."

"I know that Daniel was a beast when it came to business, but my point is, he would never pass up an opportunity for profit. Was there something wrong with the project? Did something fall through?" Sonia peered at him.

"No, nothing like that. Actually, things were

going very smoothly, he just decided to pull out." Rick shrugged. "I'm sorry I can't tell you more than that, but he didn't trust me with more than that." He glanced over at the phone as it began to ring. "Probably another fire I need to put out. Please, let me know if there is anything else you need from me." He turned away to answer the phone.

Sonia caught Nikki's hand and pulled her out of the office.

"Something's not right. It doesn't all add up." Sonia shook her head. "Whatever it is, we've got to get to the bottom of it. I'm going to start making some calls right away."

"You do that, I can walk home from here." Nikki glanced down the road. "I need some time to think all of this through."

"All right, let me know if you come up with anything. I'll let you know as soon as I find something." Sonia walked towards her car.

"Will do." Nikki smiled at her as she started down the sidewalk. Walking always cleared her mind. That was one of many reasons why she loved her job. She not only got to spend time with her favorite companions, but walking the dogs also gave her the opportunity to sort through her thoughts.

CHAPTER 15

As Nikki walked, she considered what Rick had to say. It appeared that Daniel hadn't confided in Rick. But something had rattled him. Something had made him turn away from a multimillion dollar deal with little to no explanation. Maybe if she found out what that something was, it would point her in the direction of Daniel's killer. If Daniel's actions caused Sylvester to lose so much, then maybe he was the one that she needed to talk to. Unfortunately, she doubted that he would be willing to talk. However, someone else might have something to say. She changed direction and headed for Geoff's house. As she hoped, his car was still in the driveway, though there was no sign of Sylvester's blue coupe.

When Nikki knocked on the door, she wondered if Geoff would bother to answer. A second later, it swung open, and she was face to face with him.

"Nikki?" Geoff raised an eyebrow. "Let me guess, you have some questions for me?"

"Just a few." Nikki clasped her hands together as she looked at him. "Do you have a minute?"

"Are you kidding me? In the middle of this mess that is swirling all around me, you think I have a minute?" Geoff clenched his jaw.

"I'm just curious about something that Rick Miller told me, about a man named Sylvester." Nikki studied his face for any hint of reaction.

"Rick." Geoff practically spit out the name. "You can't take anything he has to say too seriously."

"Why is that?" Nikki crossed her arms. "Wasn't he Daniel's assistant?"

"Daniel wasn't one hundred percent pleased with Rick. Rick had come to him for a loan, and Daniel didn't like that. He felt like he didn't know Rick well enough to be handing him out money." Geoff frowned. "I confronted Rick about it, and Rick denied asking for the loan. At that point, I knew that I should start keeping an eye on him."

"Keeping an eye on him?" Nikki focused in on his expression. "What do you mean by that?"

"I started documenting his activities. Daniel was a wealthy man, and I knew that attracted some unsavory folks. So, I followed Rick a little to see what he might have needed that loan for." Geoff pulled his phone out of his pocket. "And, I hit the jackpot, that's for sure." He held out the phone for her to see. "Unfortunately, I never got to show these to Daniel, or Rick would have been fired on the spot. Daniel had no tolerance for gamblers." He pointed to the second man in the photograph. "That right there, is a known bookie. I followed a hunch, that if Rick could lie to my face, then he was probably capable of a lot more than just that." He met Nikki's eyes as he tucked the phone back into his pocket. "Desperate men do desperate things."

"I'm not sure what you're trying to imply. Do you think that Rick could have had something to do with Daniel's death?" Nikki's heart pounded at the thought.

"All I'm saying is he was new in Daniel's life. Daniel started acting strange, and then he ended up dead. I can't prove that Rick had anything to do with it, but my instincts told me that he was no good from the beginning." Geoff shrugged. "I wish I had listened to them and done something straight away."

"What about Malcolm?" Nikki held her breath as she wondered how he would react to the name.

"Malcolm?" Geoff's eyes narrowed.

"Daniel's son." Nikki took a step closer to him. "You knew about him, didn't you?"

"Daniel didn't have any kids." Geoff shook his head and chuckled. "You must be mistaken."

"No, I'm not mistaken. He claims Daniel even took a paternity test. I doubt that's something that Daniel would have done without the approval of his lawyer. Didn't Daniel tell you about it?" Nikki noticed a twitch of his lips, and a faint scrunch of his nose.

"Over the years a few people tried to claim to be long-lost relatives. Of course, they wanted a piece of the pie. But none of it was real. It sounds to me like you got yourself in the middle of a hoax. If Daniel had a son, I would have known about it." Geoff chuckled. "Sorry, but you're wasting your time on this Malcolm."

"Maybe." Nikki nodded as she took a step back. She didn't see the point in arguing with him. "Is Jerome still away?"

"He is." Geoff nodded. "He'll be flying back for the funeral."

Nikki couldn't help but notice that Jerome

seemed to have conveniently disappeared around the time of Daniel's murder.

"Thanks for your time, Geoff."

"Sure." Geoff glanced past her, towards the driveway. "Mrs. Whitter and Princess aren't with you?"

"No, not this time." Nikki started down the walkway.

"You should really leave this to the police, Nikki." Geoff called out, then closed the door behind him.

On her walk home, Nikki thought about Malcolm. Was it possible that he was a liar? A con artist? If the people closest to Daniel didn't know that he existed, then maybe it was because he wasn't Daniel's son after all. Only time would tell. A paternity test would hopefully reveal the truth.

"This case doesn't seem to be leading anywhere," she muttered to herself.

As Nikki approached her apartment, she considered the possibility that Rick killed Daniel. Could he have pulled the trigger? She shivered at the thought.

Nikki stepped inside and closed the door behind her, then kicked off her shoes. Only then did she remember the sap on the bottom of one.

She rolled her eyes as she carried it over to the sink.

As Nikki tried to scrub the sap free, she recalled Petra's effort to get Bassie's paws clean. Her heart skipped a beat. Someone had to have brought the sap into the banquet room at the country club. Did they track it in on their shoes? If so, it made her wonder if Malcolm might have been there after all. There certainly were plenty of pine trees at the campground. Maybe he really was a con artist. Maybe, Malcolm had convinced Daniel that he was his father, and when Daniel found out the truth, he decided that Daniel had to go. It was hard for Nikki to believe it, but then, con artists were usually very convincing.

CHAPTER 16

Sonia spent the rest of the day making phone calls. She was certain that with enough digging she could find out some information that could help in the investigation. However, it was not as simple as she expected. Going back through decades of friendship, meant digging up some skeletons of her own. A few people were willing to talk, others still held onto grudges over simple disagreements that Sonia had forgotten about long ago. Finally, she reached a friend, who directed her to another friend.

"Call Audrey. She and Daniel were very close around that time. If anyone would know about Daniel getting someone pregnant, it would be her."

"Thanks so much, Melanie. I barely remember

Audrey. Do you think she'll talk to me?" Sonia jotted down Audrey's phone number.

"Oh yes, I'm sure she will. She has always been a big fan of yours. You may not remember her well, but she certainly remembers you."

"Really?" Sonia tried to summon a significant memory that involved Audrey. She did remember that she was often around Daniel. They'd shared a glass of wine or two. But nothing in particular stood out.

"She was always a bit shy, but she very much admired you. I'm sure she will be eager to help you out. Good luck, Sonia."

"Thank you." Sonia smiled. As she dialed Audrey's number, she hoped that she would be willing to talk. Seconds later she heard the woman's voice.

"Hello?"

"Audrey, this is Sonia Whitter, I'm not sure if you remember me but—"

"Sonia!" Audrey squealed. "Oh, what a delight to hear from you!"

"Thank you," Sonia stammered. "It's good to speak with you, too."

"It's been so very long. But I guess that you're

calling about Daniel. How sad, how very sad." Audrey sighed.

"Yes, it is." Sonia bit into her bottom lip, then took another breath. "I've discovered something that is pretty shocking to me. There is a rumor that Daniel had a child. I have no idea if he knew about the baby or not, or even if he definitely is Daniel's child."

"Oh, a baby huh?" Audrey laughed. "You didn't know?"

"I didn't." Sonia narrowed her eyes. "Is it true?"

"It sure is. Well, let's put it this way. I know that Daniel got his head turned around by a friend of mine. He got so wrapped up in her that I wouldn't hear from him for days. Then one day she just broke things off. I was surprised as it wasn't like her to be mean. I thought maybe he did something terrible, so I wouldn't let it go, and kept asking what happened. That's when she told me about the pregnancy." Audrey sighed. "Times were different then. An unwed pregnant mother wasn't treated too well, but she was determined not to tell Daniel, since he had expressed not wanting children. She thought he would feel obligated to her or desert her. She didn't want to have to deal with that."

"But Daniel would have cared for that baby. He was a good man." Sonia frowned.

"Maybe. It's hard to say one way or the other. But that was Martha's decision."

"Martha?" Sonia took a sharp breath.

"Yes, Martha Harper. They dated for about a year, but most people didn't know about it."

"A year." Sonia clucked her tongue. "No, I never knew."

"I think it was while you were busy with other things. Anyway, I'm sure Martha would have loved to see Daniel again. I haven't heard from her in a few years. Have you?"

"Not at all." Sonia shook her head. She couldn't even picture Martha. "Thanks for your help. We should get together sometime."

"I would really like that. Let me know when." Audrey's voice brightened.

"I will, I promise." As Sonia hung up the phone, it struck her just how valuable these friendships that spanned a lifetime could be. She sent a text to Nikki asking her to come over to her place for breakfast the next morning. A few minutes later she received a reply from Nikki that she would be there.

After a quick meal and some playtime with Princess, Sonia headed to bed. As she lay awake, she thought about Daniel's life. On the surface it appeared so successful, but the moment anyone looked beneath the surface they discovered a different story. There was much more to him than she ever knew.

Sonia woke up the next morning to Princess lapping at her cheeks.

"Oh dear, yes, thank you for waking me." Sonia giggled as the dog eagerly covered her face in kisses. "Good morning to you, too. Let's get you some breakfast."

Princess trotted ahead of her into the kitchen. Not long after Sonia had a shower, got breakfast ready and had Princess settled, Nikki knocked on the door.

"Good morning, Sonia." Nikki stepped inside and gave her a quick hug. Princess ran over to Nikki and Nikki crouched down as Princess leaped into her arms. "I missed you, too." Nikki laughed as Princess licked her cheek.

"Come through." Sonia smiled as she guided her to the dining room.

"This looks amazing." Nikki smiled at the selection of fruit, yogurt and pastries that Sonia had on the table. "I'm starving."

"Good, I hope you like it." Sonia smiled. "It took

a few phone calls, and some digging through my own not so stellar memory, but I figured it out."

"Figured what out?" Nikki put Princess on the floor. "It must be something good, you're grinning."

"Malcolm's mother." Sonia sighed as she sat in a chair at the table. "I was finally able to put two and two together. Knowing that Malcolm is twenty-six, I did the math, and then I was able to figure out between the tabloids, our circle of friends, and general snooping, that Daniel dated only one person for about a year. Well, one person that I was able to uncover thanks to the help of a long-lost friend. It was a bit unusual, as his relationships only lasted months on occasion, weeks was much more common for him." She poured Nikki a coffee. "Here." She set her phone down in the middle of the table. "This is her."

"She's pretty." Nikki looked at the picture for a long moment. "I can see where Malcolm got his curly hair from."

"Yes, she is pretty." Sonia leaned forward across the table and lowered her voice even though no one else was there. "Her name is also Martha."

"Martha?" Nikki looked up and met her eyes. "You mean, Malcolm's mother is the same person that Daniel sent flowers to?"

"I don't know for absolutely certain, but I figured you could tip off Quinn and see if he can confirm it. The last names are different, but that doesn't mean she didn't change her name for marriage. As far as I can piece together, Daniel and Martha were pretty serious. Then suddenly they weren't. It didn't really cause much of a commotion at the time as everyone pretty much expected him to walk away at some point." Sonia shrugged. "Looking back on it now, I realized how different Daniel was when he was with Martha. He didn't go out as much, he wasn't in the papers as much."

"Interesting. Do you think he might have been in love with her?" Nikki took a sip of her coffee.

"I guess it's possible. I didn't think he was really capable of it, but maybe whatever happened with Martha left a lasting mark on him." Sonia tightened her lips, then shook her head as she took a sip of orange juice. "Someone must have done a number on him. It might have been her. From what my friend said, she never told Daniel about the pregnancy."

"I'll send Quinn the picture. Maybe he can find out more about her." Nikki texted the picture that Sonia sent to her with all the other information she had, to Quinn. "I haven't heard much from him. He must be fully involved in the case."

"If Daniel sent flowers to Martha, it would kind of make sense that she was Malcolm's mother. Maybe, once he discovered that Malcolm was telling the truth, he decided to reach out to her. But if her house is empty, and her friend hasn't heard from her in some time, I wonder what happened to her?"

"I'm not sure, but something seems strange about it. If Daniel knew that Malcolm was his son, why wouldn't Malcolm tell him about his mother? Why wouldn't he have mentioned that she was no longer at that address? Unless she is just on vacation? But why wouldn't Malcolm tell him?" Nikki shook her head. "It's hard to piece this one together."

"One secret leads to another." Sonia rolled her eyes as she popped a blueberry in her mouth. "It always seems that way to me."

As Nikki and Sonia shared their meal, Nikki considered the possibilities. Malcolm claimed that he was Daniel's son, but they still hadn't been able to prove that. She wondered if she might get more information if she happened to stop by the police station. She was sure that Quinn would appreciate a cup of coffee, and she always enjoyed seeing him.

"Are you doing okay, Nikki?" Sonia gave her hand a light pat. "I know this has to be weighing on your mind."

"It's nothing that a good walk with the dogs can't help." Nikki flashed her a smile. "I'll be over to walk Princess with you after my rounds today."

"Great. I'm sure I'll be ready for a walk by then." Sonia patted her stomach. "Especially after this breakfast."

"Thank you for breakfast. I'm glad you suggested it. Sometimes I get so caught up in things I forget how nice it is to sit down and enjoy a meal with a friend." Nikki finished her last spoon of yogurt. "I'll see you in a little while."

"We'll be here." Sonia nodded, then looked up as Nikki stood up. "Be careful. I don't want you going off investigating too much on your own."

"Would I do that?" Nikki grinned. "I'll let you know an update as soon as I manage to track down Quinn."

"Perfect."

Nikki gave Princess a cuddle on the way out. She left Sonia's with her mind still focused on Malcolm. It seemed to her that he was the biggest change that had happened in Daniel's life. It made sense to her that he would have something to do with Daniel's murder. It crossed her mind that maybe, just maybe, Martha had something to do with his murder. Maybe that was why Malcolm didn't mention who she was. Maybe she harbored resentment towards Daniel, and when Malcolm reached out to him, she couldn't hold back her emotions any longer.

"It's possible," Nikki muttered to herself as she walked in the direction of the police station. "But where would Martha have gone?"

CHAPTER 17

*N*ikki stopped by Gina's to pick up two coffees, then headed to the police station. She pulled open the door to the station and stepped inside. It was quiet, but with tension in the air, as if everything could erupt at any given moment. She nodded to the officer behind the desk, then continued towards Quinn's office.

The officer nodded back and did nothing to stop her. Most of the officers knew her by now, not all, but most. She hoped that she wasn't pushing too hard by just showing up, but she needed to try to find out what Quinn might have discovered. She knocked lightly on the open door of his office.

"Nikki?" Quinn smiled as he looked at her.

"I brought you coffee." Nikki held up a cup.

"Aha, a coffee for an update."

"Well, maybe." Nikki nodded as she stepped farther into the office and closed the door behind her. "I figured you were pretty busy."

"Thank you, it's just what I needed." Quinn took the coffee from her. "I keep meaning to text you and then I get pulled away by something." He wiped his hand across his face. "Despite Malcolm not being willing to help, I was able to confirm that Malcolm's mother, is Martha, the woman in the picture that you sent me, and she is also the owner of the house that Daniel sent flowers to. However, no one can confirm seeing her or speaking to her in the last few weeks. She was reported missing a couple of weeks ago. We managed to bring Malcolm in for questioning with his lawyer. He stuck to his story and has no alibi. It appears that Malcolm is Daniel's son, though he was not listed on his birth certificate. He still hasn't agreed to a DNA test, but from records we can access we can see that their blood types match and there are some other characteristics that make it seem very likely." He stretched his arms above his head. "I've been stuck behind this desk all morning. I'd love to go for a walk with you. Are you due for your rounds?"

"I am, actually." They headed out of the police station and Nikki offered him her arm.

"Nikki, I keep thinking about that day. I know you say you saw nothing, but are you sure?"

"I'm sure." Nikki sighed as she looked at him. "Quinn, don't you think I want the murderer found?"

"I know you do." Quinn wrapped his arm around her shoulders. "I guess I'm just grasping at straws. Without a gun, without even a shell casing, it's hard to narrow a suspect down."

"What about the gunshot residue test you did that day on everyone?" Nikki frowned. "Did you find any residue?"

"Yes, just about every person there came back positive. Apparently, there was some kind of shooting competition right before the auction. A new shooting range had opened up at the country club." Quinn rolled his eyes. "Talk about the perfect day to plan a murder."

"Oh yes, I remember that now." Nikki paused as she glanced over at him. "Do you think it was planned? I mean, do you think someone decided to do it that day for a reason?"

"I do. I think someone had to plan ahead in order to pull it off. I don't know if things just worked out in the murderer's favor, or the murderer knew quite a bit about how the day would unfold." Quinn draped his arm around her shoulders. "At this point, Malcolm is a definite possibility, not just because of his lack of cooperation, but because he doesn't have an alibi. He will not speak to anyone, except through his lawyer."

"What about Martha?" Nikki raised an eyebrow. "I thought perhaps she had a motive to commit the crime, and she's apparently impossible to find."

"That is true. But as I said we haven't been able to locate her." Quinn shrugged. "She is still on my suspect list."

"It feels impossible to get any proper leads with this case."

"It takes patience sometimes. The goal is to solve the case as quickly as possible of course, but some just take more time. Especially in cases where the victim is well known and had many enemies." Quinn scratched the back of his neck. "Which Daniel certainly had plenty of, unfortunately. He didn't seem to mind who he double-crossed when it came to business deals."

"Did you find out anything more about Sylvester?" Nikki stopped at Coco's house to collect him. Once she had him on his leash, she returned to Quinn's side.

"Hey buddy." Quinn reached down to greet him. "There was definitely some bad blood between Daniel and Sylvester. According to Daniel's phone records, Sylvester had called him over one hundred times in the week before his death. From the length of the phone calls I would guess that most Daniel didn't answer."

"So, he was pretty much harassing him, and Daniel was ignoring him?" Nikki frowned. "Sounds like motive to me."

"It does, yes." Quinn cleared his throat.

"Sylvester was there, I know he was, I saw his car in the parking lot." Nikki hurried Coco along to pick up the next dog. Once Sassy was on her leash, she continued her conversation with Quinn. "Do you think he might have done it?"

"Well, he was there. But he has a pretty good alibi." Quinn patted Sassy on the top of her head.

"He does?" Nikki's eyes widened.

"Yes, apparently the manager of the country club prevented him from entering the banquet room, and then threatened to call the police. Geoff tipped him off to the man's presence and warned him that Sylvester would cause a disruption in an attempt to get to Daniel. I thought maybe he still could have done it, but the manager claims to have watched Sylvester drive away, and the shooting occurred only minutes later." He frowned. "It really seemed as if he had the best motive, especially since he has a criminal history."

"It's still possible, don't you think? Maybe he doubled back?" Nikki collected Ben, a Beagle, from his house as she tried to figure out how Sylvester might still be guilty.

"It's doubtful, but possible. I'll still look into him, but I think I'm better off concentrating on other suspects at this point." Quinn crouched down and patted Ben's head. "Is this all of them?"

"Yes, I'll walk Princess with Sonia later." Nikki gathered the leashes tight in one hand. It often surprised people that Nikki could walk so many dogs at once, because she was very skinny.

"How is Mrs. Whitter holding up?" Quinn matched his pace to hers.

"She is doing okay, I think. She definitely wants to find out what happened to Daniel. It seems every time we think you're getting close, there is a new suspect." Nikki glanced over at him. "I don't know how you do this every day."

"Well, I'm not investigating a murder every day.

But yes, it does get pretty exhausting, until that moment when you find that one piece of evidence that turns everything around. Then the excitement kicks back in." Quinn grinned. "That makes it all worth it."

"I hope you get to that point soon." Nikki laughed as the dogs tugged her forward.

"Me too!" Quinn jogged after them.

Sonia's patience began to wear thin as she continued to pace back and forth through the living room. Nikki had promised an update, and she couldn't wait to hear it. She'd been checking through the front window frequently for her arrival. However, it was Princess who jumped up and ran to the door before Nikki could even knock.

Sonia followed right behind her dog and opened the door while Nikki's hand hovered in the air.

"Nikki. Spill."

"I'll tell you all about it on our walk." Nikki smiled at her as she grabbed Princess' leash and clipped it onto her collar.

"Did you talk to Quinn?" Sonia stepped out through the door behind her.

"I did." Nikki detailed her conversation with Quinn as they started off on their walk. "It's a good thing you figured out who Martha was, it certainly cleared up some details of the case."

"After taking the walk down memory lane to find out who Malcolm's mother was, I realized that maybe that's just what we need to do, too." Sonia linked her arm through Nikki's as they walked back towards the house. "Maybe we need to go back to the country club, to that banquet room, and see if something doesn't shake loose from our memories."

"That's a great idea." Nikki frowned. "The only problem is, I think it's still a crime scene."

"What about Quinn? Do you think he would let us in?" Sonia met Nikki's eyes. "If he's hitting brick walls, and we are too, maybe he'll be willing to do anything to see if he can get somewhere on this case. After all, we were there when the crime took place."

"Maybe, I'll give him a call and find out." Nikki pulled her phone out of her purse and walked towards a bench on the sidewalk.

Sonia hung back to give her some privacy. She watched as a couple strolled past, hand in hand. It wasn't easy for her to imagine having someone permanently in her life, but sometimes there was a part of her that longed for it. She missed her husband.

"Sonia." Nikki walked back towards her. "Quinn gave us the go ahead. He said the crime scene has already been processed and they are releasing it back to the country club tomorrow. There's still an officer there who will allow us in."

"Perfect." Sonia smiled. "Do you want to head over now?"

"If it's okay with you. Do you think Princess will be all right?" Nikki fell into step beside her as they turned up the driveway that led to Sonia's house.

"I'm sure she will. She's been having a great time with that remote that I fished out from under the ottoman for her." Sonia laughed, and pushed the thoughts of her late husband from her mind.

"I'm glad she likes it." Nikki slipped her arm through Sonia's. "Are you doing okay? Are you sure that you want to go back to the country club?"

"I'll have to eventually. You know I can't miss too many parties." Sonia squeezed the crook of Nikki's elbow, with her arm. "I'll be fine, especially if you are there with me."

"I will be, every step of the way." Nikki flashed her a smile, then led Princess inside.

Sonia started the car, while Nikki locked the

door. Despite feeling on edge about Daniel's murder, she felt some comfort in Nikki's presence as they drove to the country club. It had been strange at first to find a kindred spirit in someone so much younger than her, but Nikki had become one of her best friends. At that moment, she couldn't imagine not having her at her side.

CHAPTER 18

"It looks pretty quiet." Sonia pulled into a spot near the entrance of the Corgi Country Club and parked. "The parking lot is practically empty."

"A murder on the property can do some damage to your reputation." Nikki frowned as she stepped out of the car. "I'm not sure how easily this place will recover from this."

"It won't be long before the golf tournaments and parties start again, trust me." Sonia followed her to the front door. "One thing that the elite are good at, is sweeping things under the rug."

"That may be true." Nikki held the door open for Sonia. "Obviously, Malcolm was swept under the rug for his entire life."

"That's if Daniel even knew about him." Sonia glanced at her. "We don't know if he did or not."

"You're right. We don't know for sure if Malcolm is telling the truth." Nikki led the way to the banquet room. An officer stood near the door, his eyes glued to the phone in his hand. "Excuse me, Officer?" Nikki paused in front of him.

"Go ahead in, Quinn gave the okay." He tipped his head towards the door. "There's not much to see, though."

"Thanks." Nikki walked past him and into the banquet room with Sonia right behind her.

Sonia froze just inside the door. The room seemed to tilt, and then rock back and forth. She grabbed the wall to steady herself.

"Sonia, are you okay?" Nikki turned back to look at her.

"I'm sorry. I didn't expect coming back here to have such an impact on me. I just need a second." Sonia straightened up. There was the podium, and the stage, and the chairs. Everything was exactly the same, aside from the absence of people.

"It's okay, take your time." Nikki gazed at her. "It's overwhelming, I know."

"I guess I didn't think it would be exactly the same." Sonia took a breath, then nodded. "I'm okay now, let's do this." She walked towards the stage. "I was right here, with Daniel at my side."

"Yes." Nikki nodded as Sonia took her position. "And I came in through the entrance with Spots." She looked back at the doors that led into the banquet room. "I'm going to try walking through again and see if there's anything that surfaces."

"Okay, I'll stay right here." Sonia stared up at the podium. "The vase," she murmured to herself. Not everything was the same. The vase that had held her attention was gone. Of course it was, it had to be processed as evidence. But its absence made it hard for her to find anything to focus on. She heard the door to the banquet room swing open, but she didn't turn to look. She hadn't heard the door that day, it had been too loud to notice it. She hadn't known that Nikki was there.

Sonia heard Nikki's footsteps as she retraced her movement through the banquet room.

"I remember looking at you and Daniel on the stage before the vase came up for auction. I was going to come see you, but I got distracted." Nikki sighed, then took a sharp breath. "I do remember something." Nikki's voice raised. "Princess."

"What do you mean?" Sonia frowned as she

glanced back at her. "I remember her, too. She was here with us."

"I know. But I remember Princess going after something on the floor, a reflection, or a light of some kind." Nikki spoke quickly, her voice wavered with excitement. "I thought it was so cute. I almost took a picture."

"I wish you had." Sonia smiled. "But what does that matter? Princess is always up to something."

"It matters because maybe it wasn't nothing. Maybe it had something to do with the killer." Nikki stared at the floor. "Are you sure that was where you were standing, Sonia?"

"Yes." Sonia looked back at the podium, then nodded. "Yes, this is it, or as close to it as I can remember."

"And Princess was right next to you, right here." Nikki walked up beside her and stared at the floor beside Sonia. "At the time I didn't think much about it, but now." She looked up at the ceiling, then over at the few high windows. "What could have made that reflection?"

"I'm not sure. Maybe one of the chandeliers?" Sonia pointed out the crystal chandeliers that spanned the room.

"No, I don't think so. At least, not on its own. It

was moving." Nikki looked up again. "It had to come from a place quite high up. Over there." Nikki pointed to the elevated seating at the rear of the banquet room.

"That's used when there is a wedding or some kind of performance. But it wasn't being used on the day of the auction." Sonia gestured at the floor to ceiling windows that flanked the seating. "I think they had the curtains closed, so it shouldn't have been light from those windows."

"No, but maybe it was something on the gun." Nikki's eyes widened. "Maybe it wasn't a reflection. Maybe it was some kind of targeting aid."

"It was a spot-on shot." Sonia frowned. "And the elevation would give the killer a clear shot over the crowd."

"Let's try something." Nikki fished in her purse until she found a coin. She placed it on the floor. "I think the reflection I saw was about here." She looked up at the seating, then walked towards it. "Which means that the murderer would have been about here." She neared the curtains, then turned to face the coin. She raised her hand in front of her as if it was a gun, and aimed for the spot. "Actually, back even a little farther I think." She stepped to the side, away from the seating and onto a step that led up to the seating. Her shoulder brushed against the heavy curtain that hung over the window.

"That looks about right." Sonia turned in the direction that Nikki pointed her hand. She could imagine Daniel standing there. She turned back to face Nikki, who had bent down to look at something on the floor.

"Look!" Nikki pointed to the floorboards on the step. "It's sap!"

"Is it?" Sonia peered down at it. "Are you sure?"

Nikki crouched down and took a whiff of the pile of goo. "Yes, definitely sap." She narrowed her eyes. "The police might have missed it during their sweep of the room, because they had no reason to be looking for it. But if my theory is right, then this is probably where the murderer stood." She grabbed the curtain that hung over the window. "He might have even been hiding behind this."

"That would explain the movement of the light." Sonia nodded as she gazed at the sap on the floor.

"I need to let Quinn know about this. If they haven't found it before, maybe there is something stuck in the sap that will give them a clue." Nikki pulled out her phone and dialed Quinn's number. "Who could have been hiding behind the curtain? Malcolm? Sylvester? Or maybe even Rick?" She sighed as Quinn's voicemail picked up. "Quinn, please call me, we found sap at the crime scene. I just wanted to let you know in case it hasn't been analyzed, yet. I'll let the officer out front know." She hung up the phone, then turned back to Sonia. "This is probably a good thing, Sonia. It means we're getting closer."

"You're right." Sonia took a deep breath and smiled. "We know where the killer was, but not who held the gun. It's a step in the right direction, but it still doesn't feel like enough."

"I'm going to tell the officer out front what we found. He can keep the evidence safe until Quinn decides what to do about it. I don't want to waste any more time. We should keep looking at other leads." Nikki narrowed her eyes. "I remember how upset Rick was when he spoke on the phone that day. Something had him distraught. He was under a lot of pressure. He could have easily snapped."

"A friend of mine is on the board that approves permits for new buildings. He told me that Geoff had recently filed for a permit for a new office complex down by the river in Magnolia. The complex was designed to house Daniel's offices as well as other businesses. He submitted a blueprint that represented a massive build." Sonia paused, and turned to look at Nikki. "If he was in the middle of this big project, then maybe something happened to the project. It would have been a huge investment on his part, so if he suddenly pulled out, that might be enough for someone to want revenge."

"Did he pull out?" Nikki pursed her lips. "Geoff said he'd been acting strangely."

"My friend didn't know for sure, but that something had stalled it, and the permit was put on hold. That was all he could tell me." Sonia shrugged. "I'm not sure what to make of it, but it might have been a crisis occurring in his life. He pulls out of a multimillion dollar deal with Sylvester and others, he stops the permit to build new offices. Sounds like a recipe to upset a lot of people."

"We can look into it more, but I think we should look into Rick first. I think I know where to go to find out more about him and what he was up to. When I spoke to Geoff, he showed me a picture of Rick and another man, apparently he is a bookie. They were standing in front of a bar. The one down by the water. We could check it out, but it might be a little seedy." Nikki cringed.

"You don't have to worry about that. I can handle seedy just fine." Sonia nodded. "Let's go.

Maybe we can find out if Rick really did have a motive to kill Daniel."

"It's worth a shot." Nikki led the way to the car. After a short drive to the bar, she and Sonia walked towards it.

"Are you sure you're up for this, Nikki?" Sonia looked at the windowless door.

"I am, if you are." Nikki took a nervous breath, then pulled open the door.

CHAPTER 19

*D*espite it being bright outside, the interior was dim, indicating that if there were windows, they were covered up with something. Sonia led the way to the bar, where a short, bald man stood behind. He rubbed a cloth along a glass in his hand and squinted at them.

"Bit early, ladies. We don't officially open for another twenty minutes."

"We're not here for drinks." Nikki met his eyes as she decided to get straight to the point. "We're here to place a bet."

"Excuse me?" He set the glass down with a firm thump. "What are you talking about?"

"See Nikki, I told you Rick didn't know what he was talking about. Forget it, we'll find someone

183

else." Sonia carefully flashed her expensive purse in the man's direction as she turned away from the bar.

"Oh, wait a minute, just a minute." A friendly smile spread across his lips. "I didn't know you were friends of Rick's. He's one of my best customers." He tipped his head towards the bottles behind him. "Why don't you two have a drink and we'll talk about placing this bet."

"Sure." Nikki's heart pounded. She wasn't much of a drinker, but she guessed it would be suspicious if she turned one down.

As he poured them each a shot, he continued to smile. "What kind of action are you ladies interested in?"

"I don't really care." Sonia accepted one of the shots from him. "I have some cash to play with, and making a big bet is on my bucket list." Sonia winked at Nikki. "So, whatever I can place a big bet on, I will."

"How big are we talking here?" The bartender handed Nikki her shot.

"Let's just say there will be plenty of zeros." Sonia looked straight into his eyes. "But I want to make sure that I place this size of a bet with someone I can trust. I heard that you can be a little harsh. I mean, I'm good for the money, but if you make a practice of threatening your customers, I'm not interested in working with you."

"Is that what Rick told you?" He smacked his hand hard against the top of the bar. "He's a liar. I've given that guy more extensions than Mother Teresa would. It's not my fault he's terrible with money, is it?"

"I guess not. But he didn't tell us, we just heard some rumors." Nikki took a sip of her drink. Her nose crinkled in reaction to the bitter liquid. "So, what is your policy if someone can't pay up?"

"It's not like there's anything in writing, but yeah, I'll put a little pressure on. Nothing physical though, I don't believe in that. You break somebody's leg, how are they going to go into work and make the money they owe you? I just keep calling, show up now and then, you know, nothing but a little intimidation."

"Intimidation?" Sonia picked up the shot and threw the contents into the back of her throat. She did her best not to gag in reaction to the burn of the liquid. "Sounds fair."

"I think so." The bartender nodded.

Sonia and Nikki both turned towards the door as they heard it open. Nikki's eyes widened as she recognized the man walking inside.

"Lucas." Nikki blurted out as he walked towards them. She recognized him from the animal shelter when he was having an argument with Grant.

"Hey, what are you doing here?" Lucas stared at Nikki.

"Just popped in for a visit." Nikki smiled.

"You know her?" The bartender asked.

"Yeah, she's a friend of Grant's." Lucas shrugged. Nikki's mind whirled with thoughts of the conversation between Lucas and Grant.

"Does Grant owe you money?" Nikki asked.

"Maybe." Lucas scowled. "What's it your business?"

"It's my business because you were at the animal shelter threatening him." Nikki tried to keep her voice even.

"Let's just say, it's not a problem anymore." Lucas smirked.

"What do you mean?" Nikki stepped boldly forward. "Is Grant gambling?"

"He used to, but just because you stop, it doesn't mean your debt can just be erased." Lucas smiled and looked at the bartender. "Luckily for Grant, my business partner and I agreed to give him a break and he has paid off his debt. So, no need to worry about him anymore."

"Are you sure?" Nikki asked.

"Yes, Grant is on the straight and narrow and everything has been cleared up." Lucas put his hands in his pockets then stepped through the door that led into the back section of the bar.

"So, about this bet?" The bartender smiled as he looked at Sonia. "There's a good basketball game coming up."

"Like I said, it'll involve a lot of zeros. As in, zero." Sonia smiled at him as she set the shot glass back down on the bar. "Thanks for the drink, though."

"Wait, don't be like that. Is it because of Rick?" The bartender groaned. "Look, he promised me he was going to get me the money. He said he'd have it for me Sunday, and then of course Sunday came and went, no money. He's been avoiding me ever since. That's no way to do business. So yes, I might have driven by his house last night. But he wasn't even home. The place was dark." He frowned. "I thought maybe he had left town. If you talk to him, you tell him, I don't play games. No matter how far he runs, he still owes me that money."

"I'll tell him." Nikki locked her eyes to his. "You're sure he wasn't there? Maybe he just turned the lights out."

"No, I'm sure. I asked one of his neighbors if they had seen him and they mentioned that they noticed him packing a suitcase and some other stuff into his car. It looks like he might be trying to disappear." The bartender narrowed his eyes. "I'm not a violent man, you see. But I do need to get my money."

"I'll pass along the message." Nikki steered Sonia towards the door.

Sonia felt a shiver run along her spine as she sensed the man's eyes still on her back. Was he calculating how much she was worth by what she was wearing? She'd experienced that more than once in her life. She felt some relief as Nikki pulled open the door and the daylight spilled over them. The person on the other side of the door made Nikki's heart skip a beat.

"Nikki?" Quinn pressed his palm against the door and held it open as they stepped through it. "What are you doing here?"

"Oh, just stopped in for a minute." Nikki met his eyes.

Sonia wobbled as she grabbed onto Nikki's arm.

"Oh dear, Nikki, it's been a while since I had a drink that strong."

"Mrs. Whitter, are you okay?" Quinn gazed at her with concern.

"I think I'm drunk." Sonia covered her mouth as she burped.

"I'd better get her home." Nikki frowned and wrapped her arm around Sonia's waist. As she started to walk away, Quinn caught her free arm.

"Are you going to tell me what you were really doing in there? I came here to talk to Rick's bookie. Please tell me that's not what you were doing." Quinn's voice rippled with tension.

"You may want to check to make sure that Rick hasn't left town." Nikki winced. "His bookie seems to think that he might have."

"Nikki, really." Quinn looked up at the bar. "That man could be dangerous. You have to be careful how you deal with people like that."

"I was." Nikki frowned.

"Maybe you could trust me to conduct the investigation?" Quinn met her eyes for a split second, then pulled open the door to the bar and disappeared inside.

"Ouch, sounds like he's a little annoyed." Sonia watched him go.

"It's all right, everyone's feeling a little tense right now." Nikki frowned. "I don't want to upset him, but this is the first real lead we've come across. If Rick really did take off, then he probably had a reason. He wanted to get away because he knew he might face prosecution."

"Or, he could have taken off because he knew that his bookie was coming after him." Sonia tilted her head from side to side. "It seems more likely to me. Why would him owing money to a bookie cause him to shoot Daniel?"

"Geoff mentioned that Rick asked Daniel if he could borrow money, and Daniel turned him down. Maybe he felt so pressured by his bookie that he got angry and decided to kill Daniel? Maybe with Daniel dead he has access to some of his money? When I heard him talking on the phone, he promised that he would have the money. Maybe he expected Daniel to give it to him that day." Nikki narrowed her eyes. "It's possible that Daniel promised him something, and then didn't follow through with it."

"Yes, you're right it is. But the murder seemed premeditated and if he's left town because he owed the money or he is worried the police are onto him for Daniel's murder, there's not much more we can find out." Sonia frowned.

"Maybe, and maybe not." Nikki lowered her

voice as she led her farther away from the bar, back towards the car. "If the bookie is right, and Rick is on the run, maybe we should try contacting him. Maybe if he knows we have this information he will talk to us and let something slip."

"I don't know." Sonia glanced back at the bar. "What would Quinn say about that?"

"I guess we'll find out later." Nikki winked at her.

"I like the way you think." Sonia smiled and climbed into the car.

"Are you okay to drive?"

"Yes, of course." Sonia winked. "I only pretended to be drunk to try and distract Quinn, so he wouldn't be upset that we were here."

"Clever thinking." Nikki smiled. Her phone began to ring before Sonia could start the engine. When she saw that it was Quinn, her heart skipped a beat.

"Hello?"

"Nikki, I'm afraid I have some terrible news."

"About what?" Nikki held her breath.

"Malcolm. He's just been found dead." Quinn sighed. "And it looks like, we also found our killer."

"What do you mean?" Nikki's eyes widened as she looked over at Sonia. "Malcolm is dead."

"He committed suicide, and left a note, that confessed to Daniel's murder. I'm headed out to the campground now to oversee the investigation. I'm so sorry, Nikki, I know this is probably upsetting, but I wanted to let you know right away. Now, you can leave this alone and stop putting yourself in dangerous situations."

CHAPTER 20

*N*ikki hung up the phone as her heart pounded.

"Nikki?" Sonia looked over at her. "Are you okay?"

Nikki explained to Sonia what Quinn had said as the bar door swung open, and Quinn ran towards his car. As he pulled away from the sidewalk, she thought about following him. "I can't believe it." She stared down at the phone in her hand. "Can it really be over?"

"If he confessed, then I'd say, yes." Sonia reached across the car and gave Nikki a warm hug. "I know you saw Malcolm, this has to be a big shock to you."

"More than that." Nikki met her eyes. "I can't believe it."

"I know, it's quite shocking." Sonia sighed.

"No Sonia." Nikki tucked her phone back into her purse. "I mean, I can't believe it. I don't believe it."

"What are you thinking?" Sonia looked back up at her.

"What are the chances that Malcolm would kill himself and confess? He had no reason to." Nikki frowned as they drove along the road towards Sonia's house.

"Fear of being arrested? Guilt over what he did to his father?" Sonia shrugged. "I'm sure there are more reasons than that."

"Something just doesn't feel right." Nikki closed her eyes, then shook her head. "Do you mind if we stop by the animal shelter? I want to see how Spots and Bassie are doing."

"Not at all." Sonia turned down the road that led to the animal shelter. "Nikki, it's important to remember that just because you like someone, that doesn't make them innocent."

"I'm not sure that I even liked him." Nikki gritted her teeth as they pulled into the parking lot of the animal shelter. "It's almost like there's a piece missing. Someone got lost in it all, and I don't know who or how." She frowned.

"Let's just see what Quinn turns up about Malcolm's death. We should find out more after that." Sonia stepped out of the car. "Let's go see those wonderful dogs. I'd love to get a glimpse of how the animal shelter has benefited from the fundraiser, too."

"I'm sure that Petra will be happy to give you a tour."

Nikki left Sonia with Petra in the lobby, then headed back to the kennels. She could already hear Spots barking. He had been so restless on the day of Daniel's murder. She still wondered if he had sensed that something was off, that someone was there with bad intentions. As she reached his kennel, he greeted her eagerly. He wagged his tail so fast that she wondered if it might fly off.

"Hey buddy, sorry I missed you this morning." Nikki opened the gate and clipped on his leash. "You know what? I could use a sleepover." She smiled as he jumped up against her legs. "You too?"

Spots nudged her hand, then licked it. He gave a soft bark combined with a faint whimper. "All right, let's see if we can make that happen." Nikki led the dog towards the lobby. "Petra, would you mind if I took Spots home with me tonight?"

"Not at all." Petra smiled. "I'm sure he'd enjoy the visit."

"I wish he could come home to stay, but there's just not enough room there." Nikki stroked Spots' back. "At least I'll get him for a little while."

"Take whatever you need from his supplies." Petra made a note on the computer, then walked around the desk. "He's been a little out of sorts ever since Sunday. I'm not sure exactly why, but something definitely has him uneasy. Hopefully, a night with you will help."

"Would you mind dropping us off, Sonia?" Nikki led Spots outside.

"Not at all, darling. I hope he gives you some comfort tonight." Sonia took a deep breath as she settled in the car. "At least we have some closure now. It explains why there was sap on the steps at the country club." She pulled out of the parking lot of the animal shelter.

"It does, you're right. Malcolm likely had sap on his shoes. I just wish I could convince myself that this really is all over." Nikki stroked Spots' fur as they headed in the direction of her apartment.

"You've been so wound up in all of this, it's

going to take some time for you to relax. For either of us to relax. I'm sure by tomorrow, things will feel different." Sonia gave Nikki's knee a light pat, then pulled up in front of her apartment. "I think we could both use a good night's rest."

"I think you're right." Nikki eased Spots out of the car, then waved to Sonia. "Talk to you in the morning."

Sonia waved back, then drove off.

Nikki walked Spots around the parking lot for a few minutes. As she did, she tried to clear her thoughts. No longer did she need to suspect Rick, or Sylvester, or even Martha. Now, maybe she could focus on spending some time with Quinn. Hopefully, with the resolution of the case he would have more time to spend with her. She hoped that would be the case. Nikki guided Spots inside her apartment and made them both something to eat. As she settled on the couch with Spots beside her, she turned on some music and willed herself to relax.

Instantly, thoughts about the investigation resurfaced. Malcolm had claimed that he was at the campground all day Sunday. No, he couldn't back that up, but had he really lied? If he had wanted to create a false alibi couldn't he have come up with something better than that?

Nikki took Spots out for one more quick walk. If there was anything that she knew for certain, it was that Daniel had a lot of enemies. But when it came to his son, he seemed to have a different attitude. Sonia felt as if he would have been thrilled to connect with him. If Malcolm really was his son, why would he go to the effort of contacting his father, only to kill him?

By the time Nikki sprawled out in her bed, her mind churned with paranoid thoughts. If Malcolm didn't kill himself, then who killed him? She tried to sleep, but as the minutes ticked into hours, the only sign of slumber was Spots' gentle snoring. She picked up her phone and checked the time. She knew that Sonia was an early riser. It was nearly six. She bit into her bottom lip as she wondered if it was too early to call her. As she considered it, her phone buzzed with a text.

You up?

Nikki smiled as she responded to Sonia's text.

Yes. Are you up for a road trip?

Nikki gazed at the phone as she waited for the response. Maybe if she went to the campground for herself, maybe that would be enough to convince her that Malcolm really had killed his father and himself.

I can be there in ten minutes.

Nikki laughed at the response, then jumped out of bed. Spots lifted his head, gazed at her with annoyance, then laid back down. She hurried to shower and get dressed, then grabbed a banana. Spots dragged himself out of bed. After he had something to eat, he followed her around, growing more curious by the minute.

"Sorry bud, you're going to have to come with, this place isn't doggy-proofed and it's too small for you." Nikki clipped on his leash and gave him a treat. As she stepped outside, Sonia's car pulled up. Nikki squinted against the headlights and tightened her grasp on Spots' leash. At the very least, he would enjoy a walk in the woods.

CHAPTER 21

With Spots settled in the back seat, Nikki and Sonia drove in the direction of the campground. Nikki watched as the sun tried to break past the shadows of the early morning sky.

"Thanks for coming with me, Sonia. I want to see the scene for myself. I know that Quinn would probably advise against it, but I just can't believe that Malcolm killed himself."

"I'm having a little trouble with that myself." Sonia nodded as she drove onto the highway. "Not only because I trust your instincts, but because he was just so young. Of course, if Malcolm isn't Daniel's killer, then the real killer would have a lot to gain from being able to stage a suicide and frame Malcolm for his father's murder."

"Yes, he would." Nikki shook her head. "I just don't know who might have done all of this. It would take a pretty cunning person to come up with such a complicated scenario."

"Or desperate. Some people become brilliant when they are under intense pressure." Sonia turned down the dirt road that led to the campground.

"That's true. I just can't shake the memory of Malcolm telling Quinn how happy he was. I believed him. He said he had everything he wanted in life. I just don't see him going from that, to killing himself." Nikki leaned back and stroked Spots' fur as the dog began to squirm on the back seat.

"Maybe he would if he felt the investigation was closing in on him." Sonia shrugged as she looked through the windshield. "Maybe he knew that he was going to lose everything and end up in prison. Someone who loved the outdoors, might find the prospect of spending time behind bars too daunting. They wouldn't necessarily be able to survive behind bars."

"Maybe you're right." Nikki frowned as Sonia parked in front of the main cabin. There was just enough light to make out the fact that the front door looked slightly open. "But I just feel like something is missing here. Malcolm killed his father after reuniting with him? Why? Daniel didn't reject him. At least not at first. He sent Martha flowers, probably as an effort to reconnect with her."

"Maybe Malcolm blamed Daniel for his mother going missing, or for her death, if she is dead, or just for her lonely life. Maybe he'd harbored resentment over the years." Sonia stepped out of the car. "I'll be honest, it feels like a stretch to me, too. I'm not sure what you hope to find here."

"I'm not sure either." Nikki sighed as she rolled her window down enough for Spots to have plenty of air, then closed the car door. "I just feel like there's something I need to see here." She walked towards the main cabin.

"Nikki." Sonia took a sharp breath as she looked at the other end of the parking lot. "Nikki, we're not alone here. Is that the blue coupe you were talking about?" She pointed to a blue car parked so far into the tree line that it was almost impossible to see it.

"It looks like it might be." Nikki narrowed her eyes. "What would Sylvester be doing out here?"

"I don't know, but we should try to find out." Sonia crossed her arms. "Now, something seems really fishy about all of this."

"You're right. I'm going to take a look inside, then we'll go check out the car. But stay close, Sonia." Nikki rubbed the back of her neck as the tiny hairs on it stood up. She tried to ignore the uneasy feeling in the pit of her stomach. Of course, it felt strange to be here, after what happened. As she started to push the door of the cabin open, her nose scrunched up in reaction to a strong smell. Something she didn't immediately recognize, but she knew that she should have. She was all the way inside the door before it finally registered in her mind.

"Gasoline." Nikki took a sharp breath and turned back towards Sonia to stop her from entering. "Sonia, stay back!"

"What's wrong?" Sonia frowned as she stepped inside as well. "Is that gasoline?"

"We need to get out of here." Nikki reached for the door, but another hand grabbed the knob before she could.

"Not so fast." The man pushed the door shut.

"Geoff!" Sonia stared at him as she took a step back. "What are you doing here?"

"I'm more concerned with why you're here." Geoff rested his hand on his hip, not far from a holster that held a gun. "I came up here early enough that there shouldn't have been another soul. And what happens? The two of you show up to interfere in my life."

"Just calm down, Geoff." Sonia held up her hands. "We can be on our way."

"I really created a brilliant plan. I mean, I really did. The thing about a good plan, is there is always a way it can go wrong." Geoff smoothed down his tie as he continued to block the door. "Right now, the police believe that Malcolm killed his father, and then killed himself, but there will always be people like you, that will keep poking until something is uncovered. I can't risk that."

"Geoff, how could you do this?" Sonia glared at him. "You killed Daniel after being friends with him for so long, and Malcolm was an innocent man!"

"I had no choice." Geoff engaged the lock on the cabin door. "Just like I have no choice now." He turned back to face the two of them. "I didn't want to hurt anyone. I really didn't. But I had invested so much of myself, my life, my time, in Daniel. I was playing the long game. I thought if I remained his right-hand man long enough, that eventually it would pay off. When he brought me in on this last deal, I decided to go all in. It was the first major deal he allowed me to join. I put in everything I had, knowing it would pay off." He closed his eyes for a split second but opened them again before Nikki could move a muscle. "Then he came across Malcolm. Or I should say, Malcolm came across him. I came out here to the cabin to speak to Malcolm. I offered him a good amount of money to drop the whole thing, to pretend that Daniel was nothing to him. But he blathered on about it being his mother's wish for him to meet Daniel. Can you imagine?" His eyes widened as he chuckled. "He wouldn't listen to reason. He was so stubborn, ironically, not unlike his father."

Nikki edged back away from him and swept her gaze around the cabin. There was one big window off to the right, and a smaller one higher up in the rear of the space. As far as she could tell, there was no rear exit.

"Once Daniel learned about Malcolm, everything changed. He wanted to pull out of the business deal. He wanted to leave every last dime of his money to his son, to make up for not being there when he was growing up. He was going to stop his plans to expand his business and retire to spend time with Malcolm. He told me to change his will and leave everything to Malcolm, and to make sure every dime of his was pulled out of the deal that we'd just made. Without his money it wouldn't go ahead. I couldn't lose everything." Geoff narrowed his eyes. "I just couldn't. I accessed his dating apps and intercepted any correspondence between Malcolm and Daniel. I intercepted Malcolm's calls, but Daniel wouldn't leave it alone. I knew the only way to keep things the way they were was to kill Daniel before he ruined the deal completely and I lost everything. That way, the deal could stay in place, and I wouldn't lose the money I invested. I could profit from something finally. I needed to ensure that the business deal would go ahead."

"Smart." Sonia nodded slowly as she stared at him. "You did have a very smart plan. I guess you even used Sylvester's car, so that just in case anyone spotted you up here, the finger would be pointed at him. What I'm not sure about is, how did you get Malcolm to write that confession?"

"I didn't. When I found him, he was pretty close to wanting to end things anyway. He'd lost his mother, and his father, and was suspected of committing his father's murder. I convinced him that if he wrote the suicide note, I would fake his death, and he could go on to start a new life in a new place and leave all of the pain behind him. All I had to do was add a few words to make it a confession as well." Geoff winced. "I really didn't mean to ruin the kid's life."

"Wait a minute." Nikki stepped closer to him. "Martha's body hasn't been found. No one knows for sure if she's dead."

"Oh, I do." Geoff smiled sadly.

"You killed Martha, too?" Sonia gasped. "But why?"

"She started calling Daniel. She wanted to warn him about Malcolm knowing the truth, I guess. Anyway, I intercepted the calls. I went to visit her. She didn't mention Malcolm, but said there was something very important that she needed to talk to Daniel about. I knew it was likely some kind of money grab. So, I arranged for an accident to happen. She was out for a hike one day, and she just happened to slip off the edge of the trail. I never expected that no one would find her." Geoff shrugged. "But that really worked out in my favor, I suppose. Unfortunately, Daniel discovered one of her calls, and then he tried to make contact with her. He called her, sent her flowers on a couple of occasions. He got distracted by trying to contact her. So, you can imagine how panicked I was when Malcolm came looking for him. Unfortunately, Malcolm managed to contact Daniel before I intervened." He sighed. "Really, I did all of this for Daniel."

"No, you didn't." Sonia glared at him. "You didn't do a single thing for Daniel. You did it for your own greed. You're a cold-blooded killer, and you're going to pay for what you've done."

"Maybe." Geoff smirked as he looked at her. "But not before I add two more bodies to my list of sins." He glanced at his watch. "I came up here to burn the place down, just in case I left any trace of evidence here. It spooked me a bit when the police found that sap at the country club. I thought I had covered my tracks well. But I missed something. It must have gotten stuck to my shoe while I was visiting Malcolm. Anyway, I'm not going to make that mistake again. So, this place, has to go." He raised an eyebrow as he gazed at them. "The only question is, will anyone know that you went with it?" He pulled a lighter out of his pocket, then twisted the lock on the door. In the same moment, he pulled out his gun and pointed it at Sonia. "Either of you move a muscle, and the other one dies." He shook his head. "I'm sure that neither of you want to be responsible for that." He kept the gun pointed at Sonia as he stepped out the door, then pulled the door closed behind him.

"We have to get out of here!" Nikki ran for the door and pulled at it, but it wouldn't budge. "He's got us trapped!" She ran towards the large window on the side wall just as the first flames began to leap around the front door.

"He must have lit it from the outside." Sonia hurried over to Nikki. "Can you get the window open more?"

"No." Nikki pried at it. "It's stuck in this position. There's not enough room to fit through."

"Okay, we'll break it." Sonia pointed to the desk near the door. "Can we lift that? We can throw it through the window."

"I think it's going to be too heavy." Nikki and Sonia tried to lift the desk, but it didn't budge. "Let me try this chair." Nikki grabbed a chair from against the back wall of the cabin and began to swing it at the window. The legs bounced off the glass, as the flames spread around the exterior of the building. "We're not going to be able to get out through there now." Nikki coughed as she backed away from the window. "Get low, Sonia, the smoke is getting thick."

Sonia grabbed Nikki's hand and pulled her down beside her.

"There has to be a way out of here."

"I'm going to call for help." Nikki pulled out her phone, but as she tried to dial, the call was rejected. "I don't have any service. Do you?"

"My phone is in the car. Help won't get here soon enough. This place is going to go up fast." Sonia coughed.

"There's another window, but it's small. I don't think either of us will be able to get through it." Nikki ran her hand along the rear wall of the cabin. "Maybe we can find a way to get through the wall?"

"The wood is too thick." Sonia shook her head. "And everything is covered with gas. We need to get away from the walls, they will burn so hot." She led Nikki into the center of the cabin.

"There has to be a way out." Nikki did her best not to breathe in too much smoke as she peered through it. The front door was engulfed in flames. No one knew that they were there. The campground was empty. No one would notice the fire for some time. Far too late to save them. Her heart sank as she realized that this time, they really were trapped. She wasn't going to be able to find a way to get out. Already her lungs burned from the smoke. Beyond the crackling of the flames, she heard a whimper, and a loud bark. "Spots!" Nikki gasped. "He's still in the car."

"I don't think he can get out of the car. If he can get out I'm sure he'll stay away from the fire." Sonia hugged her. "Right now, we need to focus on getting us out of here."

"Sonia, I'm sorry, but I don't know how we can escape." Nikki wiped at her eyes as tears slid down her cheeks, both from the hopelessness of the situation, and the smoke that made her eyes water.

"Now, now." Sonia hugged her tighter. "There is never a good time to give up."

Nikki's heart pounded as she realized that Sonia was right. She couldn't just sit there and wait for the smoke and the fire to overtake them. She had to do something, even if it was pointless.

CHAPTER 22

ikki grabbed two cloths on a shelf beside the desk, then walked into the bathroom. Although there was no window, there was a sink. She turned on the water and soaked the cloths, then handed one to Sonia.

"Put this over your mouth and nose, maybe it will help."

Nikki used the other cloth to cover her mouth and nose. As she searched through the bathroom for anything that might help, she wondered how long it would be before anyone even noticed the fire. She guessed that there was a good chance it could be hours.

"Maybe we should try to get through those

flames." Sonia looked at the front door. "It's starting to fall apart. Maybe we can get through it."

"I don't think we can." Nikki frowned. "I don't think we would survive it."

"There has to be some way!" Sonia crouched down near the floor. "The smoke is getting so thick!"

"Someone will come for us." Nikki did her best to sound convincing. As she began to repeat her words, she heard the slam of a car door. "Someone's out there!"

"Nikki!" Quinn's voice pierced through the roar of the flames. "Nikki! I'm coming in!"

"Quinn, don't!" Nikki winced as the flames on the walls jumped higher. "It's not safe!"

Loud barking startled Nikki as it came from right behind her. She turned to find Spots.

"Spots! How did you get in here?" Nikki bent down to hold him, but he wriggled out of her arms. "No, Spots, no!" She gulped as she watched the dog run straight for the flames. Before he reached them, he slid down into an opening in the floor.

"What's that?" Sonia coughed as she inched forward.

"I'm not sure, but if Spots was able to get in that

way, that means there must be a way out." Nikki looked over at Sonia. "It's our only hope!"

"Let's do it!" Sonia nodded as she grabbed Nikki's hand.

The two crawled towards the opening in the floor. The trap door had been pulled open from underneath. Nikki could only guess that Spots had managed to tug it open.

"You first." Nikki guided Sonia down through the opening.

"It's tight, like a crawlspace." Sonia called back. "But I can see light! Hurry, Nikki!"

Nikki dropped down into the crawlspace right behind her. As she followed Sonia, she could feel the heat from the fire above them. Sirens wailed, it sounded as if they were right outside.

"There's a way out, Nikki." Sonia looked back over her shoulder, then crawled forward and out into a small opening.

Spots barked as he spun around in circles, trapped in the small space, which was surrounded by stone.

"What is this?" Nikki patted Spots.

"It must be some kind of cellar, maybe it can be used for food storage, or firewood." Sonia peered up at the top. "I'm not sure we can climb out."

"Quinn!" Nikki shouted as loud as she could. She doubted that he would hear her with the sirens being so loud, and the roar of the flames loud as well. "Quinn!" She managed to pick up Spots. She stood up on her toes and reached up in an attempt to lift him out through the hole. Sonia tried to help as well by pushing him up. But he was too heavy, they couldn't quite reach. Nikki put Spots back down on the floor and turned to Sonia. "You're going to have to get on my shoulders."

"Nikki, I'm not sure I can do that." Sonia frowned.

"You can. I know you can. We can't stay here, if the flames get any worse, we won't be able to survive in this small space." Nikki crouched down. "Use the wall to steady yourself. Once you're on, I'll stand up very slowly, and you should be able to reach the top."

"I'll try." Sonia took a shaky breath as she kicked off her shoes. She put one foot on Nikki's shoulder, then grabbed the wall. As she brought her other foot up onto Nikki's other shoulder, she gasped.

"Go slow, Sonia, take your time." Nikki grabbed her leg to help steady her. "Are you ready for me to stand up?"

"Yes, I think so." Sonia shifted her feet on Nikki's shoulders. "Okay, go ahead."

Nikki stood up as slowly as she could. She strained against Sonia's weight, despite how petite she was. She vowed that she would take up weightlifting as she did her best to remain steady. She doubted she would have enough energy to lift her without the adrenaline that the dire situation caused.

"Can you reach, Sonia? Can you pull yourself up?"

"I don't think that's going to be a problem, Nikki!" Sonia called out with laughter and relief in her voice.

"Hang on, Mrs. Whitter, I'm going to pull you up." Quinn's voice drifted down to Nikki's ears. She closed her eyes against tears of relief as she felt Sonia's weight lift off her shoulders.

"Nikki. Are you okay?" Quinn leaned over the edge of the opening.

"I'm okay." Nikki nodded as she gazed up at him. "Here, do you think you can reach Spots?" She held the dog up to him.

"I think I can." Quinn eased his body along the edge and reached down for the dog.

Nikki raised up on her toes and with all the strength she could muster she shoved Spots higher.

"Got him!" Quinn gulped as he snatched the dog out of her hands.

Spots gave a furious bark, then flipped around in Quinn's arms and licked his cheek.

"Okay, okay, enough." Quinn wiped at his face as he put the dog on the ground. Sonia crouched down to pat him. "Now you, Nikki!" He reached back down for her.

"It's too high, Quinn." Nikki shook her head as she looked up at him. "You won't be able to pull me that far."

"We've got you." A fireman appeared at the opening. He dropped down a looped rope in her direction. "Just put that around you, and we'll have you out of there in no time."

Nikki pulled the rope over her and looked up as the fireman and Quinn began to pull her up. Quinn met her eyes and didn't look away, until she was out of the hole. Then he wrapped his arms around her, with the rope still on her.

"Nikki, I'm so sorry, I couldn't get through the flames."

"Quinn." Nikki hugged him as her heart finally began to slow. "You saved me. You saved us."

"I think that honor belongs to Spots. I couldn't believe it when I saw him jump through the car window to save you." Quinn laughed as he looked down at the dog that jumped up against his legs and barked at him. "Let's get you both checked out by the paramedics." He kept his arm around Nikki's shoulders and wrapped his free arm around Sonia's. "I'm sure you took in a bit of smoke."

Nikki rested her head against his shoulder and sighed. "How did you even know we were here, Quinn? How did you find us?"

"I showed up at your apartment with an early breakfast. I was investigating this further. Malcolm's suicide seemed too convenient. It didn't all add up. I wanted to properly discuss your thoughts on Malcolm's confession. I thought maybe I was missing something." Quinn squeezed her shoulder. "But you weren't there. So, I went by Sonia's, and her car was missing. I knew there was only one place you would sneak off to, the campground, because you believed Malcolm was innocent."

"Quinn, I'm sorry, but Malcolm was innocent." Nikki looked around in search of the blue coupe. "It was Geoff, Geoff was here. He killed Daniel, Malcolm, and Martha." She coughed as she attempted to fill in the details.

"We'll get to all of that later." Quinn met her eyes. "Right now, you need to do what the paramedics tell you to do."

"Okay." Nikki sat down in the back of an ambulance, with Sonia across from her.

Sonia reached for her hand. "We made it, Nikki."

"Yes, we did." Nikki squeezed her hand. "I vote for never getting trapped in a fire again."

"I second that." Sonia coughed and laughed at the same time.

After the paramedics were satisfied with the state of their lungs, Nikki and Sonia were both allowed to leave the ambulance.

"Where's Spots?" Nikki glanced around between the firefighters and the police officers.

"I think Quinn has made a new friend." Sonia smiled as she pointed to the dog, huddled close to Quinn's legs. As Quinn turned and walked towards them, Spots followed right behind him.

"We were able to pick up Geoff." Quinn glanced down at the dog that jumped up against his leg. Then he looked up at Nikki. "He went back to his house, which is exactly where we found him. I'll need your statements, but once he found out that you survived the fire he confessed. I think he knows there's no way for him to get out of this." He gazed into her eyes.

"I'm sorry." Nikki frowned as she looked from him, to Sonia. "I never should have come out here and put us both in danger." She met Quinn's eyes again. "If it weren't for Spots, and you, I don't think we would have made it out of there."

"Try not to think about that." Quinn hugged her. "I just want to get you and Sonia home, so that you can rest."

"That sounds wonderful." Sonia ran her fingers through her hair. "And maybe I can wash some of this soot out of my hair."

"Would you mind dropping me off at the animal shelter, instead?" Nikki reached down to pet Spots. "I think this guy needs a bath, and lots of treats."

"Nikki, I really think you should rest. I'll take care of Spots." Quinn leaned close. "Can you trust me to take care of him?"

"Absolutely." Nikki smiled as she gave him a quick kiss.

ot long after Nikki stretched out in her bed, she realized that she couldn't sleep. Despite having no sleep the night before, and going through quite a harrowing experience, all she could think about was Spots, and whether he was okay. Had Petra taken him to the vet? Did he breathe in too much smoke? Finally, she gave up, and headed out the door. As she walked to the animal shelter, Dahlia felt different to her. The tension of Daniel's murder had broken. The killer had been found, and three murders had been solved. People could relax again. She could too, once she knew that Spots was okay. The walk was quite long and once she reached the door of the animal shelter she felt relaxed. She headed inside, eager to see Spots.

"Petra? Are you here?"

"In the back." Petra called out. She stepped into the hallway. "Aren't you supposed to be resting?"

"I just wanted to see Spots." Nikki smiled. "He's my hero, and I want to make sure that he's okay."

"Oh." Petra shook her head. "Nikki, he's not here."

"What? But Quinn was supposed to drop him off." Nikki frowned. "Are you sure?"

"I'm sure. I thought he was still with you." Petra shrugged. "I'm sure he's fine if Quinn has him."

"Yes, you're probably right. But I still want to know where he is." Nikki frowned as she left the animal shelter. Would Quinn think she was checking up on him? She didn't want to hurt his feelings, but she needed to know where Spots was and that he was okay.

As Nikki walked to the police station, she tried to think of all of the reasons that Quinn might not have taken Spots back to the animal shelter. Maybe something came up with the case? Maybe he left him at the police station?

Nikki waved to the officer at the front desk, then

walked back towards Quinn's office. As she knocked on his open door, he looked up at her.

"You're supposed to be resting." Quinn quirked an eyebrow.

"And Spots is supposed to be at the animal shelter." Nikki crossed her arms as she looked at him. "Where is he?"

"Oh well, I did take him there." Quinn cleared his throat. "I mean, I pulled into the parking lot."

"Okay?" Nikki stared at him.

"But then I thought, maybe I should take him to the vet first. You know, Petra's busy, and she might not be able to get him to the vet. So, I took him to the vet, and don't worry, he's fine. The vet checked him all out." Quinn smiled.

"That's wonderful. Thanks for doing that, Quinn. But where is he now?" Nikki narrowed her eyes.

"Well, then I thought, Spots did such a good job. He deserved something special. So I took him to the pet supply store, and he found this bed that he really liked, and a few toys, and I picked up some food for him." Quinn shrugged. "I think he had a good time."

"Wow, you spoiled him, I love it." Nikki grinned. Then she shook her head. "But where is he?"

A loud bark emitted from behind Quinn's desk.

"Shh!" Quinn whispered. His eyes widened as he looked up at Nikki.

"Quinn, is Spots back there?" Nikki walked around the side of his desk, and saw the dog, curled up in a brand-new bed, surrounded by toys. His tail wagged when he saw Nikki.

"A few toys?" Nikki laughed.

"He deserves them." Quinn cleared his throat.

"Yes, he does." Nikki crouched down to pet Spots. "Do you want me to take him back to the animal shelter for you? I'm sure you have paperwork to do."

"No!" Quinn frowned. "I mean, yes, I do have paperwork to do. But I don't want you to take Spots back. In fact, if Petra will let me, I would like to adopt him." He met Nikki's eyes as she looked up at him. "Do you think she will? I know with my work hours she might not think it's a good fit."

"Oh Quinn!" Nikki's heart felt so full she thought it might burst. "Of course, she will. I can help you when you're busy with work."

"I just couldn't take him back there, Nikki, not after he saved you and Sonia. I know Petra takes good care of the animals, but he needs a real home." Quinn crouched down to pet the dog as well. "Do you think it's a good idea?" He looked up at her with a sheepish smile.

"I think it's a wonderful idea." Nikki leaned close and kissed him.

Spots barked, then began to lick both of their cheeks.

"Hey now!" Quinn laughed as he scratched behind Spots' ear. "I don't think he wants to share me."

"Well, he's going to have to." Nikki wrapped her arms around him and smiled.

The End

Christmas Chocolates and Crimes

Hot Chocolate and Homicide

Chocolate Caramels and Conmen

Picnics, Pies and Lies

Devils Food Cake and Drama

Cinnamon and a Corspe

Cherries, Berries and a Body

DONUT TRUCK COZY MYSTERIES

Deadly Deals and Donuts

Fatal Festive Donuts

Bunny Donuts and a Body

Strawberry Donuts and Scandal

Frosted Donuts and Fatal Falls

NUTS ABOUT NUTS COZY MYSTERIES

A Tough Case to Crack

A Seed of Doubt

Roasted Penuts and Peril

DUNE HOUSE COZY MYSTERIES

Seaside Secrets

Boats and Bad Guys

Treasured History

Hidden Hideaways

Dodgy Dealings

Suspects and Surprises

Ruffled Feathers

A Fishy Discovery

Danger in the Depths

Celebrities and Chaos

Pups, Pilots and Peril

Tides, Trails and Trouble

Racing and Robberies

Athletes and Alibis

Manuscripts and Deadly Motives

Pelicans, Pier and Poison

SAGE GARDENS COZY MYSTERIES

Birthdays Can Be Deadly

Money Can Be Deadly

Trust Can Be Deadly

Ties Can Be Deadly

Rocks Can Be Deadly

Jewelry Can Be Deadly

Numbers Can Be Deadly

Memories Can Be Deadly

Paintings Can Be Deadly

Snow Can Be Deadly

Tea Can Be Deadly

Greed Can Be Deadly

Clutter Can Be Deadly

BEKKI THE BEAUTICIAN COZY MYSTERIES

Hairspray and Homicide

A Dyed Blonde and a Dead Body

Mascara and Murder

Pageant and Poison

Conditioner and a Corpse

Mistletoe, Makeup and Murder

Hairpin, Hair Dryer and Homicide

Blush, a Bride and a Body

Shampoo and a Stiff

Digging for Dirt

WENDY THE WEDDING PLANNER COZY
MYSTERIES

ABOUT THE AUTHOR

Cindy Bell is a USA Today and Wall Street Journal Bestselling Author. She is the author of the cozy mystery series Wagging Tail, Donut Truck, Dune House, Sage Gardens, Chocolate Centered, Macaron Patisserie, Nuts about Nuts, Bekki the Beautician, Heavenly Highland Inn and Wendy the Wedding Planner.

Cindy has always loved reading, but it is only recently that she has discovered her passion for writing romantic cozy mysteries. She loves walking along the beach thinking of the next adventure her characters can embark on.

You can sign up for her newsletter so you are notified of her latest releases at http://www.cindybellbooks.com.

.

Made in the USA
Middletown, DE
15 August 2019